THE DEVIL'S DONE COME BACK

THE DEVIL'S DONE COME BACK

NEW GHOST TALES FROM NORTH CAROLINA

Edited by Ed Southern

—BLAIR—

Printed in the United States of America
Cover design by Ashton Smith
Interior design by April Leidig

Blair is an imprint of Carolina Wren Press.

The mission of Blair/Carolina Wren Press is to seek out, nurture, and promote literary work by new and underrepresented writers.

We gratefully acknowledge the ongoing support of general operations by the Durham Arts Council's United Arts Fund and the North Carolina Arts Council.

The stories in this book are works of fiction. As in all fiction, the literary perceptions and insights are based on experience; however, all names, characters, places, and incidents are either products of the author's imagination or are used fictitiously. No reference to any real person is intended or should be inferred.

Library of Congress Cataloging-in-Publication Data
Names: Southern, Ed, 1972- editor
Title: The devil's done come back : new ghost tales from North Carolina / Ed Southern.
Description: Durham, NC : Blair, 2025.
Identifiers: LCCN 2025022781 (print) | LCCN 2025022782 (ebook) | ISBN 9781958888650 paperback | ISBN 9781958888728 ebook
Subjects: LCSH: Ghost stories, American—North Carolina | Haunted places—North Carolina—Fiction | North Carolina—Literary collections | LCGFT: Ghost stories
Classification: LCC PS648.G48 D48 2025 (print) | LCC PS648.G48 (ebook)
LC record available at https://lccn.loc.gov/2025022781
LC ebook record available at https://lccn.loc.gov/2025022782

Contents

A House of Vine and Shadow

PART ONE—LIVE OAK

Nate Batts half expected the door to crumble when he knocked.

Shoot, he half expected the whole ramshackle house to collapse, so derelict it looked, so forlorn did it sag. Through his boots he could feel the porch boards give like sponges, and his nerves began to jangle against the excellent chance they'd crack and cave underneath him. God only knew what muck, what creatures, he'd be among then.

He could tell this once had been a trim little farmhouse, and before that a sturdy dogtrot cabin, somebody's pride and joy. Whoever had built or pieced it together had to have done so with skill, care, and self-respect, or else it wouldn't still stand at all. No, this house's only fault was sustained neglect. Vines long since had overtaken both front corners, not kudzu but honeysuckle, wild cherry, and strawberry runners, and what looked to be some kind of grapevine, maybe scuppernong. Nate decided that yes, it was scuppernong, because he wanted it to be. Rot webbed the window casings, and up the porch columns ran cracks as thick as the vines. The whole house listed to the west where erosion had steepened the yard's natural slope, and, of course, the porch and door seemed ready to crumble if Nate breathed too hard.

Aside from all that…

The first crew they'd sent to survey had assumed this house was abandoned. Nate's bosses' guy in the county office had shocked him by saying that according to the last census, an old couple still lived there.

"Unless they've died since then and no one's discovered them yet," the county man had added.

Nate hated this part of his job: not the prospect of finding two corpses, though that pleased him none, but the prospect of finding two living people, living here. He hated being the point man for developers he'd never met and never would, money men set to make more money by turning more of the North Carolina countryside into one more high-end subdivision full of "luxury" homes that looked like they were made of cottage cheese, like they were imitation castles in a cheap amusement park, overstuffed with overlarge rooms and garages, bristling with too many peaks and gables. Whatever shape it now was in, this house here had been prettier than what his bosses would build, more fit for a home, once upon a time.

He looked back over his shoulder at the highway the road crews already were widening, the country road already becoming a commuter trail, feeding the growing city that once, not that long ago, had been far away. He assumed that whoever lived or had lived here once had grown tobacco in the skinny fields surrounding the house, between Highway 234 and the tree line of pine: He still could see the rolling swells of the furrows. Soon they'd come to level those rolls of red earth, to clear those pines, to culvert the branch that ran in their shade.

He hated that, hated his part in its happening, hated that this was the job he'd fallen into once he'd set out to join the building trade. Nate had wanted to follow in the footsteps of his grandfather, who'd come home from World War II and framed houses, framed so many so well he could send his son to college and his son could send his grandson. That work had seemed to Nate something to take pride in, and he'd wanted to do work that was something like it. He'd thought this job would be such. He'd thought wrong.

This was his job, though, and his bosses paid him well to do it.

Nate turned back to the door, fist raised to knock again.

Nate Batts about jumped out of his skin.

The door stood wide open, and the old man staring at Nate from its maw looked like a living skeleton, except for his one eye cloudy and his one eye a deep and earthy brown.

"We been waiting on you an age," the old man said.

Nate's jaw dropped, and a sound fell out, somewhere between a mumble, a gasp, and a gulp. All he could see behind the man was shadow.

"Well, don't just stand there letting the flies in now that you're finally here," the old man said as he turned away. He shuffled a step or two into the dark of the house, then nodded, not quite looking back.

"Oh, right," he said. "Won't you come in?"

Nate would have been more alarmed but less confused if the old man had called him by his Christian name. As it was he couldn't quite rule out that the old man did know him, and wasn't just senile or blind or both. If the coot had called him "Nate" he'd have had better reason for the sense, deep down and not yet nagging, that he was being lured to some kind of doom.

He tried not to follow. "Sir? Sir? Sir, I'm from the Goldleaf Company and I . . . and I . . ."

He stood with his toes on the transom, leaning from side to side as if he could better his view.

"Sir? Sir?"

Nate stepped inside, talking fast so that he wouldn't have to face silence as well as the shadows.

"Sir, I'm with the Goldleaf Company, my name is Nate Batts, and are you the owner of this property, 'cause if so we'd like to make you an offer on this property, an offer we have faith you'll find..."

Nate had stepped into what he could only call a parlor, lit by an oil lamp and wallpapered with yellowed newsprint. Along the far wall, beneath a picture window curtained on the outside by honeysuckle vines, was a high-backed, high-armed sofa, and on the sofa sat the old man, next to an old woman, both of them smiling and expectant. Their skins were the same gentle, faded brown of... well, of gold leaf, of tobacco well-cured, so that Nate couldn't tell if they were white or Black, Hispanic or Native, or a mix of some or all such categories. Maybe they were Lumbee; Nate had known a few in college. The old man had that one eye a deep brown, but the old woman had two of the brightest blue eyes he'd ever seen.

Those blue eyes fairly sparkled as she said, "We're so glad you're finally here."

"I... our..."

"Oh, won't you take a seat, please?" She gestured at the wall she faced, the wall behind Nate, and the wingback chair waiting against it.

"Uh, no, I..."

The woman kept smiling, but different somehow, and Nate could've sworn she said something, but he couldn't make out a single word.

"Thank you," he said as he settled into the cushion.

Nate was about to say more, but he never would have believed the woman could rise and leave the room with such speed. He looked after her into the shadows for a dangling moment.

"She's been like to have a fit waiting on you to get here," the old man said.

Then the woman was at his side, reaching down a mason jar of brown liquid into his hand.

"How about some tea?" she said.

The ice inside clinked like a ring of jangling keys. Some part of Nate's mind was able to think, *Well of course it does, seeing how bad her hand trembles.* He snatched for the glass before she dropped it and spilled the tea all over him. Only then was some part of his mind, maybe the same part, able to think, *But I never heard it clink at all until it was there, until she was there beside me. I never heard her foot step or a floorboard creak, neither.*

The tea was delicious, though, so sweet he'd have sworn he could feel his teeth start to come loose from his gums.

"Thank you, ma'am. As I was saying, I'm Nate Batts from the Goldleaf Company, and we're going to be putting in a new development right here along this stretch of the highway. Now, we've already purchased every other lot in this tract—I'm happy to show you the property map, if you'd like—and we're prepared to make a more-than-fair offer on yours. Now—"

"Oh, that sounds lovely," the old woman said.

"Yessir," the old man said, "a fair price is all I ever asked for, and is hard enough to find. Can't turn down a deal if it's *more* than fair."

"Uhh..."

This was not how this usually went.

"Oh," the old woman said, "but we might ought to tell him first, though."

"Likely so," the old man said. "He looks stouthearted enough."

"Yes, we ought to tell him. He ought to know beforehand."

Nate said, "Beforehand?"

"I reckon he ought to. He probably don't believe in such anyway."

"I believe he'll believe soon enough."

Nate said, "Believe?"

The old man reached out a bony hand, and Nate could've sworn the hand kept reaching, kept coming, long after it should have had to stop. He could've sworn he could see the bony fingers about to brush his face, though the old man still sat across the dark parlor.

The old man said, "Before we go any further—before we can leave this place and keep our consciences clear—we need to tell you a story."

"Oh, foot, dear," the old woman said, "he needs to hear more than the one story."

The old man clucked his tongue. "Well, but they're all the one or the other story, ain't they?"

"How about you just get to telling and let him decide?"

The old man exhaled. Nate could've sworn he saw smoke fill the room. He inhaled because he had to, but instead of smoke he filled his nose with something rich and bittersweet, with a little of the rot of pluff mud, a little of the sting of salt. One breath of that scent and he felt a sharp wind strike his face and gray sand give way beneath his toes.

His nose must have wrinkled and his eyes must have narrowed because the old man smiled at him and said, "That's the live oak."

Nate nodded, even as he wondered, *What live oak? I've seen no live oak here.*

The old man stopped smiling. He put his bony hands on his knees. Nate wished he would stop looking at him like that. He tried to look away, to look at the old woman beside him, to look down at his glass of iced tea, but found he couldn't.

"Everybody tells some story of their own creation," the old man said. "Every one of them's at least a little lie, but God forgive those whose story's too much a lie, and God have mercy on those poor souls who forget entirely even the lies.

"Some such stories tell of battles fought or havens sought, some of magic treasures found or secret gardens discovered. Some tell of murders most foul, brother killing brother, or of con jobs or kidnaps or other crimes.

"What kind of a place, though, and what kind of a people living in it, start their story with the lost, the lost and never found, never found because of what the finding might mean? Start with the lost and move on to the outcast, the effluence, the runoff, and the villain laying low? What kind of a place, I ask you, and what kind of a people?"

Nate could feel his eyes wide as he stammered, "I . . . Goldleaf . . ."

The old man said, "Now listen—"

Girl, Dare, Doe

—AMY ROWLAND—

GIRL

My name is Virginia, but I'm from North Carolina. In school we watch the film about Virginia Dare, "the first English baby born in the New World." She was born in my state, on Roanoke Island. We have the same birthday! August 18, but she was born in 1587.

She was the original Virginia from Carolina, but the teacher says back then Carolina was called Virginia—crazy confusing!

VIRGINIA DARE

God knows why it seemed like a good idea to put a pregnant woman on a boat from England to the Graveyard of the Atlantic. But Granddad was the governor of the new colony, and he did Walter Raleigh's bidding. He also wanted to set an example, helping recruit folks by bringing his pregnant daughter and her husband to homestead in the new land. After unloading, the little fleet headed back to England for more supplies. Mama said Granddad didn't want to go. He wanted to stay and be governor. But none of the other colonists would get back on the ship, and they begged him until he agreed to go.

That's the story I was told anyway. He left days after I was born, and I never saw him again. The locals offered to help us plant corn and pumpkins, but the colonists rejected them, rather sniffily, Mama said. The women sometimes accepted venison on the sly. The locals were just plain better at hunting and field dressing.

DOE

It starts in October, the killing. Once the hunt has begun, it cannot be stopped. The hunter lives in preparation and hates a fruitless search.

GIRL

I see them from the school bus. Their trucks are pulled over, between the road and the trees. The beautiful deer is tied on the dog box with his tongue hanging out. The men are standing around the tailgate puff-faced and proud. Dad says not to be sentimental. It's hard not to be sad when you drive ten miles behind a truck with a bloody deer staring at you with dark dead eyes.

DARE

The story was that they sailed back to England for supplies and couldn't return for three years because of war with the Spanish. There were also some who didn't want to come back. The whole outfit was pretty disorganized. When they did finally return to the Outer Banks, a nor'easter hit them in the inlet and several men died. The rest refused to go ashore until the captain demanded it. First they overshot it, and then they got distracted by a fire down the beach. Granddad's diary says when they reached the spot where he'd left us, he found the letters CRO carved into a tree, and the name CROATOAN carved into a post. He believed we had moved south to Croatoan—they call it Hatteras now.

DOE

The hunters travel in small herds. They want to think it is a tremendous skill, and it's true, some are better than others. But hunting us is about the easiest thing in the world. Some hunt with dogs, but a lot of them go into the woods and spread corn on the ground and climb into their deer stands. They sit there and relax; some of the younger ones mute their phones and play video games. When we walk under the tree, they shoot.

GIRL

I run outside when they pull up. Mama is calling after me that I'm still wearing my nightgown and to grab a robe and not to slam the screen door. I'm glad they don't have a deer with them. I love to watch them unload the dogs from the dog box if there's no dead deer on top. My dad's hunting friend lifts the lid of the box where they store things, and I see the stickers about guns and the second amendment. One sticker says THE VIRGINIA DARE SOCIETY.

DARE

They never made it to Croatoan, even though it was only fifty miles away. They were so close! There was another storm, and after some squabbling, they up and sailed back to England. My mother and I were abandoned by her father, my grandfather. We were not lost; we were abandoned. The legend is that those 116 of us left behind . . . well, there are loads of legends. Some say we were attacked and killed, some say by the ones who were here first, some say by the Spanish. Some say we starved to death. Some say we were lost at sea. The bad thing about being a ghost is all the nonsense you can't dispute. Prime example: I was transformed into a white doe by a witch doctor. Nope.

DOE

It is passed down. Some details change; some things depend on the teller. But the story is roughly the same from year to year. First, avoid them. We know where the hunting camp is, and the things they do there. We know the skinning tree, where the unlucky are strung up, unstrung from their bodies. We know how they track, how they kill, how they stand around and pat their faces and slap their backs and exclaim their pride, which they so often mistake for honor.

GIRL

"What's the Virginia Dare Society?" I ask the man who owns the dog box. "I'm Virginia, too," I say. "Virginia was a good girl," he says. "She vanished," I say. "She died before she was damaged goods," the man says, and my father calls the man's name sharply. "What?" I say. "What does that mean?"

"She was turned into a white doe," the man says, "and she died a virgin."

"What's a virgin?" I ask.

"She hasn't been touched by a man," he says, and gives me an odd look.

"Huh," I say.

"You be good," he says. "You're Virginia the virgin." I don't like this man. "Virginia," Dad says, "go get out of your nightgown and put some clothes on."

DARE

Oh for goodness sake. They love me because I was abandoned and left for dead and turned into a white doe and loved by two Indians, one who decided to kill me and one who decided to save me? They struck me simultaneously with an oyster arrow and a silver arrow so that I turned back into a swooning maiden who died a beautiful bloody virginal death? Please. Americans should leave mythology to the Greeks and Romans.

DOE

We are born the size of babies but can stand within thirty minutes and outrun a man within three weeks. We often have a twin because both of us probably won't make it. From the beginning, we know how to be very, very still. Predators can see us, hear us, and despite the misinformation that we have no odor, smell us. We hate that we have to hide, but necessity makes us expert.

GIRL

My dad doesn't hunt with the man anymore. Mama asks him why, but he shakes his head and goes outside. She looks at me and shrugs. "Men," she says.

DARE

They left us to die. They knew we would eventually, after they lost interest in looking for us. A historian said the "great governor" John White, my grandfather, who abandoned us, must have "assumed we were happy." I learned a lot in my short life, and I've learned more in the centuries since death, and one of the few certainties is never to assume people are happy. I could have been. My own family and neighbors made sure that didn't happen.

DOE

It is passed down. The hunter enters the woods. The only one who knows the woods better than the hunter is the hunted. It is hard to live in fear. Fight or flight. Live ready to flee. Fleet of foot. You must be faster than the slowest. That is the unspeakable, born in our bones, that we must outrun each other, our own family members. When the hunt starts, someone will be killed, if not today, tomorrow. Would you rather it be you, your mother, your brother, your own offspring?

GIRL

The dog-box man ran away with the Jacksons' daughter. The hunters went searching for him. It was like they were leaving for a hunt in their trucks with guns and dogs. I watched from my bedroom window. They came back two days later. The man is with his wife again. I saw them at church with their baby. Jasmine, the girl he took away with him, is grounded. She has to stay home. She only comes outside to do chores and go to church.

"Why is Jasmine in trouble?" I ask. "Why isn't the man grounded?"

"Men can do what they want," Mama says. "Not girls. You better remember that. If you ever run off with anybody, I'll kill you myself."

DARE

It was years later. We had survived somehow, with help from the Croatoan that the colonists had to accept even though they hated it. (We did move there, as planned, and were easy to find if anybody had bothered to look.) I was bathing in the creek, and he was fishing nearby, although I didn't see him that first day. I came up on the bank shaking the water from my hair and found a beautiful trout on a bed of oak leaves beside my shoes.

We saw each other after that, glimpses at first, through the leaves, then from a distance across the field, then from behind a water oak, then the day he stood very still in a clearing and looked at me steadily until we both smiled ourselves silly.

DOE

I only had one this year, and she was dead by September. It's a sad job losing all these young. My oldest son heard and came back to visit. The other does are jealous—they usually don't return once they leave. But he came to pay his respects. He is a dear, that one, and he's turned into a lovely young buck.

GIRL

I was in the hunting shack. It had been gutted long ago, everything not nailed down taken. The only things left in the room were the hunting regulations my dad tacked to the wall with duct tape, a few candle nubs melted into jar lids, an old army cot, and some chairs that were hard-worn and smooth-bottomed. I could see the oak branch that touched the window when the wind blew. I was alone; it was my secret reading spot. I saw the dog-box man coming closer through the woods, through the quiet trees, making the leaves shake. He was coming, quickly, quietly, like a hunter. I was afraid. I slipped out the back and hid in the woods. I could see him standing in the doorway. "Come here, little doe," he said, and laughed. He called again and drank from his beer bottle and laughed his ugly laugh and shut the door.

DARE

We had plenty of time to die. But we weren't that special. The Lost Colony like the Lost Cause is a romantic story for those inclined to a certain strain of nostalgia. People disappeared here regularly, all sorts of people, for centuries. We weren't the first or the last. Some got sick, some starved. And then there was the massacre when I went to live with my beloved.

DOE

They shot my son! I have to find him, see him, let him know I'm here.

GIRL

I went to the library to find out more about Virginia Dare. The pictures at first seemed nice. She was pretty, dressed all in white. I read a story by the Virginia Dare Society about how Virginia Dare was the birth "of the white race in the Western Hemisphere" and read some more stuff that I didn't understand. I asked the librarian what scientific racism was. She told me. She's a nice lady, but she don't sugarcoat. I was so upset I forgot to check out my deer book.

DARE

Of course they need their purity symbols because they are so degraded. People are people everywhere, but people who can't accept or even acknowledge history are doomed. My memory is murky; it's a problem for ghosts. You think it's hard to remember where you put your keys? Try wafting around without a body for four hundred years. I know I loved a man and that I wasn't turned into a white doe and killed by a jealous Wanchese "who hated the English." It wasn't like that at all, but it gets all jumbled. I'm remembering now. That means a mood is coming on. It's torture, the voices in the wind. They said something when they came for me. What was it?

DOE

I go right up to the house. Let them kill me if they want to. He is here, my son, hanging from the skinning tree. My son! I lick his eyes closed and look at his blood in the bucket and wish I could tear their house down. Instead I eat their flowers, every single one. I hate mums. I hate them, and I eat them until I am sick.

GIRL

I wait for them to come home from the hunt. The deer is strapped on top of the dog box. He's a pretty one, but a little small. "He's small," I say, and the hunters who have been laughing turn to me and go red in the face. "He's big enough!" He is strung from the skinning tree, his throat cut, the blood sloshing out of the bucket staining the grass. They have to be bled first so they won't taste gamey. I ask mama if that's for true, and she says that has nothing to do with it. "It's an old wives' tale," she says.

"But how can men tell old wives' tales?" I ask.

"Believe me," she says, "men tell the biggest old wives' tales of all."

DARE

Let me set this straight at least. I remember this. When I moved into his house—they had nice houses with rounded roofs and manicured paths and tall cedar pole fences—the colonists came for me. They came not to save me but to kill me. You know how in *The Searchers* John Wayne is unstoppable in his search for Natalie Wood, who's gone off with the Comanche and been "contaminated"? (Yes, ghosts have movie nights; we watch through windows.) When you first see it, you're like oh, John Wayne, the big mister who will stop at nothing to rescue his niece. Then you realize he's hunting her to kill her.

DOE

I am being sick by the side of the house when I look up and see the girl in the window. She's in the lamplight, a half-feral-looking thing with long wild hair and a curious face. She waves at me. I look at her and consider. She can't help it if she lives with killers.

I look at her, and she smiles and opens the curtain wider.

GIRL

I sit at the living room window, calling softly to the doe. I don't want to wake Mama and Dad, so I am very quiet. I turn on the lamp, so she will see me looking friendly. She's here! She is right under the window, and I hold the curtain wide. "Hello," I whisper. She looks at me, then behind me, and freezes. I turn to see what she's looking at. Oh no, oh no.

DARE

"Do you want to get him killed?" his mother asks.

"No, I say. I love him."

"You are bringing death here," she says, but I don't listen. She is right.

They come, my family, my neighbors. They have guns. "Death before assimilation!" they shout, before the slaughter.

DOE

My father's head is mounted on their wall. I run, crashing through the woods, crying and puking mums. I want my son's body. I want my son. I am going to gather the does and ask them to charge the place, to take my son's body back.

GIRL

She looked in the window and saw the deer head on the wall. I feel so bad. She must hate us. I go see Jasmine, and she tells me what happened at the hunting camp. It was spooky in there, and she wanted to leave, but he wanted to play a game. "What sort of game?" I say.

She shudders. "He wanted me to be a white doe. That's what he called me, his little white doe." She starts to cry.

"Don't cry, Jasmine," I say. "I'll protect you. I know where the guns are."

DARE

I am in the field when they take my son and slaughter his father and most of the others. I hide in the woods. I don't know what to do, so I walk all night, and then I turn around. I want my son.

DOE

The earth is stained around the skinning tree, and that's the truth of it. Does telling a story depend on words? I don't think so. Look in the trees. That's the story here, always has been. It's right there. The things we've seen that have taken place in these woods, in these trees. We are not the only creatures they have chased through the trees with dogs and rifles.

GIRL

I sneak out of the house. I have to find the doe.

DARE

I sneak through the village. I have to find my son.

DOE

I sneak through the woods. I have to find help.

GIRL

The things in the trees.

DARE

The things we've seen in the trees.

DOE

The things we've seen in these dark creaking trees.

The Lulling of Blackbeard

—HEATHER FRESE—

Edward Thatch—Blackbeard the Pirate; six feet, four inches tall; billowing black beard; wild eyes—stopped short in the hallway of the sprawling plantation house on mainland Carolina, his boots nearly crushing the shadowy cat that had not been there a moment ago.

It had not been there a moment ago. He knew this.

Edward placed a callused hand on the wall, unused to the way the floors and walls stood still, unaccustomed to the lack of tilt, the absence of slapping waves on hull. Unaccustomed to the lull.

It was late June of 1718, the Carolina air thickly humid. Edward Thatch had sworn off piracy and would marry in the morning.

The cat glared at him with cold emerald eyes, rasped a hiss-meow, and vanished.

Edward Thatch—Blackbeard the ferocious, Blackbeard the brutal, Blackbeard the most feared pirate of the Atlantic—stood in the hallway, unsettled, marrying in the morning, the ghost of the ocean under his feet.

Mary Ormond—sixteen years old, sharp-eyed, willowy but for a nascent roundedness to her stomach—stood with tear-streaked cheeks on a precipice overlooking Bath Creek. With a sob that heightened in pitch to a scream, Mary reached up and yanked yaupon leaves out of a hunched, gnarled tree, ramming them into her father's satchel. In love with a boy who'd been banished to sea, brokenhearted at her impending wedding to Edward Thatch, infuriated that her father had brokered her to a *pirate*, Mary ripped and pulled until her palms bled, bright drops glistening on the satchel's worn leather, redder than yaupon berries in the sun. Mary shoved down a last handful of deep green leaves, breathing hard, shaking, her dress whipping in the salty breeze.

Beneath Mary's feet, the roots of the yaupon tree coiled into the sandy North Carolina soil, vibrating with power. The water of Bath Creek splashed higher, penetrated with the salt of futility, pervading every cell of her body, washing into the dividing cells of her child. The drops of Mary's blood slipped off her father's satchel and onto the sand where they dissolved among the nestled stickyburrs.

It was late June, 1718. Mary Ormond was getting married in the morning.

Edward neatened his beard for the wedding, the slick metal of the shaving blade chill in his hand. His face in the mirror darkened as that damn cat appeared again, glaring up at him. Something about the cat's haughtiness, its audacity and swagger, put Edward to mind of Governor Eden. Governor Eden who, in a show of power, had offered him a pardon when the legalities of privateering took a turn to piracy, that nasty word.

One month ago, Blackbeard had dominated the city of Charleston, blockading the harbor with his ship, the *Queen Anne's Revenge*, and the seven others in his flotilla. He'd captured Charleston's elite, threatening to behead them if his demands were not met. Blackbeard enjoyed the heft of the sword hilt in his hand, holding his blade to their pliable necks.

His demands were met, of course, because he was Blackbeard. He'd released the bastards, minus their clothing and personal effects. Then, swollen with his victory, he'd sailed his beloved *Revenge* into a sandbar, splintering her hull, rendering her feeble as the laws of piracy tightened around him. Trapped, with embarrassingly little treasure, he'd agreed to the governor of North Carolina's pardon and terms. Trapped to an upright life of decency, marriage, and the mainland.

The morning of Edward's wedding, stifled power streaked through his body, and Edward kicked at the cat with a roar, but the cat had already disappeared. Had it been there at all? Plumes of anger sparked around his head as he slicked the shaving blade across his face one last time.

In a small room across the house, Mary had been laced into stays, her shoulder blades nearly touching. Her swollen breasts rounded the top of her wedding dress's square neckline, a pinner of linen and lace capping the coils of her hair. She was a girl in the year of our lord 1718, and as such, she would obey her father's command.

One month ago, Mary had straddled her lover in a dense thicket of yaupon that was their meeting place, rocking her hips, harboring the secret in her body that would bind her to him. She'd enjoyed the slickness of their bodies, the way the stubble of her lover's chin caught strands of her hair and stretched them like spider's silk. Mary whispered her secret into the curve of her lover's ear and rolled off his body. "Shall we marry?" she asked.

Her request was unmet, of course, because she was a girl in 1718. Mary's father, irate at his daughter's situation, deemed her lover unsuitable and ran him out of town. Wan with defeat, Mary had stood at the dock, watching her beloved sail toward the line of horizon. Trapped, splintered, powerless, she'd agreed to her father's terms. The governor needed someone to bind Blackbeard to the mainland. Her father needed the governor's favor. Mary's unborn child needed wedlock. No one thought about what Mary needed.

The morning of Mary's wedding, terror and helplessness gusted over her skin, raising goosebumps. Mary scooped up her shadowy cat and met its eyes in the mirror.

If one could peer into the church that June day in 1718, one would see the slightness of Mary beside the bulk of Edward. One would hear the crack of thunder as the sky opened into a summer storm while Mary and Edward woodenly repeated their vows. One would note a white-hot streak of lightning sizzle through the sky at the first touch of their hands.

In the kitchen of the plantation house, the yaupon leaves Mary had pulled lay spread to dry on a piece of linen, vibrating, power concentrating in their veins, white-hot. Deep in Mary's body, though she did not know this yet, a seed of power had taken root and would begin to course through her veins as well.

At the altar, Mary dropped her hands from Edward's and glared at her father, terror evaporated. Seething.

At the altar, the ocean thrummed in Edward's ears. Calling him.

If one could sail down the trickling creek that widens to a wide gush of river as it flows from the mouth of Bath, then sail across the coursing waters of the Pamlico Sound, one would find the thin island of Ocracoke arced in the Atlantic Ocean. A barrier island, Ocracoke's geological function is to protect the mainland.

If one could follow the drop of Mary's blood drawn from the yaupon as it joined the soil, one would see it seep deep, Ocracoke's protection pulling it past the roots of jimsonweed and water hellebore, deep under the creek that widens to a salty river, deep beneath the muck of the Pamlico Sound, until it rises to the arc of Ocracoke's protective coastline. Ocracoke, an island that has withstood the pounding of waves for centuries, for centuries protecting the mainland. You would see Ocracoke, standing powerfully in the face of the late June storm.

"I'll not share your bed," Mary said to Edward, the words rising unbidden from her throat on their wedding night. She'd been unlaced from her stays and stood in their bedroom in her chemise.

He towered over her. "You'll do as I wish." But Edward Thatch lay still beside Mary Ormond as if a shimmering line of protection had been erected between them. He'd never raped, for women came to his bed of their own volition. He had lovers in port cities from Tortuga to Providence. On principle, Thatch forbid his crew the crime and would unencumber them of manhood if they disobeyed.

In the same bed, Edward and Mary slept. Outside, wisps of fog gathered along the ground, cicadas whirred, and the fragrant white petals of jimsonweed blossomed open, turning their faces to the moon.

Mary awoke the next day craving yaupon tea. She slipped out of the bed where Edward slept and walked to the cooking house, the shadowy cat winding around her ankles. The spines of the yaupon leaves pricked sharp against Mary's fingers, and as she sifted and boiled and brewed, she had a thought—the flora of the Carolinas held power. Held poison.

Startled by the idea, Mary released the yaupon and ran through the plantation's grounds, not stopping until she reached the folded white trumpet curves of jimsonweed. She would scour the woods later for water hemlock.

By mid-July, Mary Ormond had thrice attempted to poison Edward Thatch. The once-imperceptible swell to her stomach had grown to a small knot, and Mary's panic rose daily at the thought of bearing a child under his eyes.

But Blackbeard would not die.

"Husband," Mary said. "Your tea." With a nod, with downcast eyes, Mary placed a cup in front of Edward. She knew from her three previous attempts how ridiculously fragile the scattered pink flowers on thin porcelain looked in his meaty fingers.

Edward's beard had regrown thick and full, and as he drank the tea, he shook his head as if to clear water from his ears. Shortly, a dull buzz would ricochet in his skull, and Edward, only mildly poisoned, would storm out of the house, stalking to town where his crew had begun to assemble, one pirate at a time.

Mary dared a glance at him. Her cat jumped on the table and hissed, back arched.

"Damn that cat," Edward thundered. He slammed the cup on the table's wooden planks, the thin porcelain cracking, delicate flowers opening.

A new idea wafted from the cup and into Mary's body. She studied the table with knitted brow, then looked to Edward. She placed a gentle hand on his shoulder. "I worry for you, husband, for I see no cat."

August is a month of thick heat in coastal North Carolina, and Edward Thatch could no longer resist the call of the sea. He could no longer stay in that house with Mary and her shadowed eyes, never knowing when her damn phantom cat would pounce, claws out. The constant thrum of cicadas in the yaupon trees drove him nearabout mad. His crew had taken over the port of Ocracoke, despite rumblings that Governor Eden and Virginia's Governor

Spotswood were in cahoots to clear their coasts of pirates, and that the Royal Navy was now engaged. Edward's crew had plenty of rum and no fear. Edward, mindful of the rumblings, commandeered a few ships quietly, tucking them in Ocracoke's harbor.

Ocracoke was not unaware of this.

Blackbeard—now Blackbeard once again, fearsome, powerful, in command of the sea— sailed back to Bath, upright citizenship, and his new wife. Her shadowed eyes and that damn cat.

Mary, during the weeks Blackbeard was on Ocracoke, walked the woods and swamps relentlessly, culling nightshade, horse nettle, and her favorite, the white, sweet-smelling curves of jimsonweed. Energy coursed through her body even as her stomach grew heavier, as she sorted, dried, steeped, and brewed.

Ocracoke was not unaware of this and whispered the names of plants through the ground. Plants to cloud his vision this time, to keep her pregnancy secret and safe. And lover's flora. Ocracoke began beckoning Mary.

In a graveyard near the plantation, the plants grew. Mary gathered them. She would banish the pirate one way or another.

In September, the humidity evaporated from the air. The skies over Bath were radiant blue, and golden waving reeds lined the creek. Mary tied back her hair and bent to wash her hands of her latest harvest. The swirl of the creek felt so pleasant that Mary impulsively undressed and bathed, enjoying the flow of water across her rounded midsection. When Blackbeard's footfall thudded along the precipice, Mary did not startle. Instead, she turned to him.

At the sight of the Mary's swollen breasts, heat shot through Blackbeard. He had never raped, but he'd been too preoccupied recently to carouse. "What are you doing, woman?" he asked.

Mary raised her chin. "The water is fine, husband," she said. "Tell me of Ocracoke."

Blackbeard stared, then sat on the bank. Compelled to speak as if the words were being drawn from him, he told Mary about Spotswood and Eden, about the rumors swirling like rum in the rain. He told Mary about the ships he'd commandeered, which crewmates had bedded which women on Ocracoke, how he'd begun to gather ammunition and to polish his sword.

Mary stepped from the creek, naked. Crossing her arms over her chest, she slowly walked to her dress, picking it up with languid arms. Ocracoke pulled her, called her, a line of taut energy she knew to follow. She turned to address him over her shoulder. "Next time, you will take me."

Her hips rolled as she walked back to the house.

Blackbeard's body was a lightning rod.

By October, Blackbeard was wildly unsettled. Lulled by Mary, excited by Mary, confounded by Mary, unable to take her by force, his defenses shaken, cicadas and ocean waves whirring in his ears, the cat swiping at him when he least expected it, Blackbeard, despite how unwise it was, craved the sea to the point of insanity. As he craved Mary's body. There was no one with whom to carouse in Bath that October evening. He stalked from town through fog and darkness to the plantation and staggered into the bedroom and his wife.

Mary had been sleeping, but she half woke as his heavy body hit the bed. He smelled of rum and sweat and soiled fabric, his beard matted.

"Wife," he said. "Bed me."

The current of energy from Ocracoke to Mary's body heightened, buzzing, and she thought, *You will go to sea and never re-*

turn you will go to sea and never return you will go to sea and never return. In her body, Mary felt her baby move, as if signaling that she needed to be on that island to draw him away for good. "Take me to Ocracoke. Then you may."

From another room, the cat shrieked a meow. Mary pretended not to hear.

The next morning dawned gray and murky, and Mary served Blackbeard his tea, infused with aphrodisiacs and poison.

Blackbeard drank, stood, spat, hurtled the porcelain cup across the room. "Bilge," he roared.

You will go to sea and never return you will go to sea and never return. "Perhaps the yaupon for tea grows cleaner on Ocracoke," she said, taking up a broom. "Take me there," Mary said.

The cat materialized, stalking a circle around Blackbeard's legs. He kicked it away, and Mary pretended not to notice. At that moment, the escape of waves crashing in his skull called him more strongly than lust. He rubbed his blurred eyes. "You will remain on land."

At the port of Ocracoke, on Blackbeard's newly commandeered ship, the pirate and his crew drank and sang and fought. Governor Spotswood's boats began their journey down the coast. Mary roamed the land, gathering, gathering. She stilled her search each day in the graveyard. Low clouds scudded across the graying sky, and a chill wind lifted her hair.

It was late November of 1718, and Mary slipped her latest concoction into a bottle of rum, gathered her cat, and climbed aboard Blackbeard's boat, unseen. She'd had enough trying to lure him, enough playing games, enough enough enough. She would bear him no longer.

Blackbeard, though cognizant of Spotswood's fleet, was too

unsettled to stay on land another minute. His men arrived, and with a tip and a tug the boat floated down the creek, to the river, to the sound. When she sensed they were in the midst of the Pamlico, Mary placed down her cat and whispered it to torment the pirate. Mary waited.

The boat slid into Ocracoke's harbor; rope thunked on the wooden dock. A blaze rose in Mary as the island and the girl it was protecting coalesced. She climbed to the deck, the ocean breeze cascading over her face. She inhaled, then stepped across the boards until she spotted Blackbeard.

Blackbeard—six feet, four inches tall; Blackbeard, riddled with poison and aphrodisiacs; Blackbeard, blurred and wild of eye—was staring down at the cat. "Tell me you see it," Blackbeard said.

Mary pretended the cat did not exist. "Oh, my husband," Mary said, leaning forward, bosom heaving, "I am not here." She stretched the bottle of rum toward him, and he compliantly took it and drank. *You will go to sea and never return.* Mary turned, walked, hips swaying. Around her, the pirates began their melee.

If one could look down to the narrow stretch of Ocracoke Island that November evening, one would see how the boat swayed with the beat of the pirates' feet and the blaze of Blackbeard's mind as the accumulation of Mary's dosages drove him to insanity. One would feel the boat vibrate with Mary's rage and power. One would see Spotswood's fleet rounding the curve into Ocracoke's harbor as night fell, taking Blackbeard by surprise, carrying a young sailor called Maynard who was itching to rid the coast of the pirate plague.

Blackbeard threaded candles into his beard and struck a match, the sulfur scent curling around his head. He set sail with a roar, a pulling of ropes and a splashing of water on hull until his ship pulled alongside his enemy, tying off to them. Blackbeard and his crew boarded their ship in a cacophony of metal and smoke and screams.

Mary strode to the deck. Ocracoke offered coursing power, and Mary channeled it. Despite her rounded midsection, she climbed to mid-mast, agile as a cat.

Blackbeard, the heft of his sword heavy in his hand, swung and swung. Spotswood's men shot him, once, twice, three, four, five times, but still Blackbeard swung his sword. Maynard disposed of a pirate crewmate and swung to face Blackbeard.

Mary, ablaze with power, shouted, "Husband!"

Blackbeard, hearing her call, turned his head. Maynard struck and with a heave, sliced it off. He lifted Blackbeard's head by its hair, high in the air. Blackbeard's mouth gaped open, his wild eyes dead.

Blackbeard's body, however, coursing with months of poison through its still-flowing veins, strode toward where he'd heard Mary's call. Blackbeard's body, still moving, reached for her, desperate to quench his desire.

From the mast, Mary cursed, "*You will go to sea and never return!*"

Blackbeard's body, headless, obeyed, but as he dove into the sea, he swam around his boat three times, still in search of his wife, before sinking to the bottom of Ocracoke's sandy depths.

Mary, wind in her hair, power in her veins, climbed down the mast. She gathered her cat in one arm and raised the other to the star-coated Ocracoke sky, issuing a full-throated cry in thanks for the island's collaboration. Mary Ormond was sixteen years old, gloriously widowed, gloriously strong, gloriously free.

The Midwife

—MICHELE TRACY BERGER—

GREAT DISMAL SWAMP, NORTH CAROLINA: 1859

The midwife needs to find her way back to the boats. Jojo and Bonalee should have been right beside her, but they got separated during the fighting. Her chest aches from running, spittle flies from her mouth. Heaving, she ducks behind a pine tree, crouches, and glances back. She strains to hear footsteps, notes the morning peep of a sparrow. The sounds of dawn don't soothe her as the smell of burning flesh is still fresh in her nose. The streaks of bright blood on her hands remind her of a reckoning only half finished.

She bites her lower lip. The many men who accompanied her are doing the work she set them to do—destroying the camp of Death-Talkers. *I told them about the shortcut, made them repeat it back to me.* Even with clear directions she knew how the swamp could play tricks on you, how easy it was to get lost. Trapped spirits all knotted together here, too, that one had to watch for—slave, free, Indian, and white.

A branch snaps nearby, and she moves on, despite the fiery pain in her knees. This part of the swamp is filled with gum trees, easy to get tangled up in their roots, so she moves with care. The baby swaddled against her breast stirs. The midwife adjusts the sling, places her left hand on the newborn, and quietly hums to comfort it.

Her mind flashes on all the babies and children of the camp that could never be saved. *Can't help them. Evil's in them already.* She saved only one, and that was dumb luck. This one. Miraculously, alive and unharmed. To save just one baby from doing their bidding. What *they* did there. *Babies born only to serve the darkness.* Her brown face with yellow undertones tightens, and a catch pinches her side. *What I did there. Helping those girls deliver their babies. But I didn't know that's what I was bringing them into this world for. Babies just come, they don't know right from wrong! Lord, I didn't know. Let us make it right today.*

What would her family say if they knew? Everyone already thought she was odd for risking life and limb helping the runaways and the others with their babies. If the whites in town got wind of what she was doing in the swamp, even as a free Black woman it would be certain death. *Without trial or jury.* The midwife shudders, barely avoiding a tangle of roots thinking about what could be done to her.

She remembers the first day visiting the strange camp run by a man and woman, foreign but white. Women and girls of all backgrounds lived there. Some people travel to the swamp to disappear, so she did not question the gathering. She took care of the women and helped them deliver their babies. It was only after many months did she wonder why she never saw the same woman or her baby again. "They left," the woman growled at her once with a ferocity that chilled her. After a routine delivery the midwife pretended that she was leaving the camp, but instead she hid nearby. It was the newborn's screams that startled her from sleep. The woman held the baby, and the man stood over them chanting words. He then shouted, "Speak to us, great spirit!" For a brief moment, the baby stilled and to the midwife's surprise spoke the words, "I am here." A triumphant look crossed the man's face, but just as soon it became a scowl as the baby began to cry. "Don't leave us. Stay in the body," the woman begged. The baby wailed and continued to wail as the woman shook it. Whatever had been called forth was now gone. In a fit of rage, the man snatched the baby, twisted its neck, and threw it to the ground. The midwife's body clenched. The couple walked off. The midwife had seen enough. They were sacrificing the newborns to bring something wicked forth. She named them the Death-Talkers, ones that clawed spirits from the other side to possess the purest of bodies. On that day she plotted to destroy the camp.

There weren't many clumps of thickly wooded forest in this part of the swamp, but she now passes through such a strip. Trees so tall and dense she could see only a sliver of sky above her. Just a little farther and they would be waiting for her.

She realizes a moment too late that she has stepped on a rotting pawpaw. The decaying speckled-colored fruit carpets the ground. In a flash, she loses her footing. Instinctively she wraps her arms tight against the baby and tries to land on her side. Once down, the midwife fails on the first attempt to get up. Her hand squeezes a clump of leaves searching for a rock or stick to steady her. Taking a labored breath, she sits up, muck clinging to her. The baby is wailing. Every part of her body feels run down and used up. During the fall, items tumbled out of her bag: glass bottles that are homes for salves and herbal oils, herb sachets, and, most important, her knife. Eyeing everything she shakes her head. She was supposed to have time to bless the earth after dispatching the evil of the camp. *No time. Others will have to come back.* Grabbing the knife, she forces herself to stand and continue walking.

After a few minutes of quieting her breath, she spots three canoes along the edge of the shore. The still crying baby announces their arrival, and the waiting men and women spring into action.

Her eyes shine as she breathes a sigh of relief. Scanning the group, she sees Jojo's slender body among them, and a spark of warmth spreads across her chest. *Good.* They probably have already made the wards. We can come back later to fortify. *Good.*

Pushing through despite the pain, she picks up the pace. The ground underneath her rumbles. A scream erupts from one of the women named Ruth, standing next to a canoe. Ruth points and shouts, "Flora, watch out."

Flora sees what is rising from the ground, from tree stumps, and from beneath the submerged roots of the ancient old cypresses. She shivers and every muscle in her body tenses. Grayish bloated bodies of what were once babies and children appear across the landscape. Vaporous crayfish tails protrude from sockets that once held eyes. Their heads move in unison, crayfish tails wiggling, as she nears the boats.

"Get in the water," Flora screams, waving her hands.

A man shakes his head "Bonalee? The others."

"We can't wait. Go, go, go."

Crayfish erupt from everywhere along the sandy shoreline. These humped rat-sized crayfish are not like any Flora has ever seen before. As several men push one of the boats in the water, her heart gallops in her chest. An army of crayfish multiply like ants and swarm over them. Their pinchers fly across the skin of her friends, tearing, ripping off chunks. Chaos breaks out among the remaining people. Skidding, Flora switches direction and runs toward the second canoe. "Leave," she shouts, her throat dry and raw.

The ghosts of the babies hover above the land.

She reaches the boat, hands grab her, pull her on. A searing pain engulfs her back that shocks her entire body. She feels her flesh being scraped away—all she can register are the claws and bites being inflicted on her head, neck, and back. Flora hears the scratching and scrabbling of the crayfish in the bottom of the canoe.

There are too many of them. With her last bit of strength, she pulls the baby out of the sling and thrusts it into a pair of hands beating and pulling the vile creatures off of her.

A blurred male face looms in front of her and frowns. "What are you doing?"

"Take her and go," Flora says, heaving herself off the canoe. The frowning man heeds her and with the baby hops out of the second canoe and wades out to the third one. He hands the baby off and pulls himself in. The paddlers of the third canoe make haste.

Flora hears the baby's cries as she is dragged down into the sand.

The Maco Light

—EARLY, JUNIPER, AND WILEY CASH—

The rain had stopped a few hours earlier, but the highway leading west out of Wilmington was still wet. Inside the car, ten-year-old twins Pearl and Tiffany sat in the back seat, their father in the front alone. From back there, the twins could hear him tapping his wedding band against the steering wheel to the beat of whatever song came on the radio, and from where Pearl sat behind the passenger's seat, she could see light brush against the dull gold of her father's ring as it tapped in rhythm. It was October, and dusk gathered itself around the car like a cold blanket. But inside the car the three of them were warm and excited.

Along with their classmates, Pearl and Tiffany had been assigned the task of researching old North Carolina ghost stories. The students in the class had been paired off, and because Pearl and Tiffany did everything together, it went without saying that they would do this project together as well. The story they'd been assigned to research was about a mysterious phenomenon called the Maco Light.

According to legend, the bluish light that often appeared where the old railroad tracks once ran through the small community of Maco was the light by which a ghost had been searching for his lost head for nearly a century. The headless ghost, whose name in life had been Joe Baldwin, had worked as an engineer for the Norfolk

Southern Railway, which ran between the port cities of Norfolk, Virginia, and Wilmington, North Carolina. One night, after the train was stopped by a tree that had fallen across the line, Baldwin had been on the tracks in the darkness when another train, unaware of what lay ahead of it, pinned him between it and the train that had stopped for the tree. Baldwin's head was severed during the accident, and he'd been looking for it ever since. According to countless sightings, on some nights, visitors to the now-missing tracks could spy the ghostly blue light of Baldwin's lantern swinging in the distance as he roamed the woods, searching for his head.

Pearl and Tiffany didn't know whether or not the story was true, and they hadn't been able to find anything online about anyone named Joe Baldwin, but there were just too many eyewitness accounts to deny that a blue light was often visible at night in Maco.

"I've seen it," their principal Miss Baden said one day. She'd found the girls sitting beside one another on the couch by an overflowing bookcase in one of the school's hallways, thumbing through various books of ghost stories.

"What did it look like?" Tiffany asked. She closed the book she'd been reading and set it on her lap.

"Just a blue light, kind of hovering in the distance," Miss Baden said.

"Did it ever get close to you?" Pearl asked.

"No," Miss Baden said. "It just stayed where it was, and then it disappeared."

"Do you believe it's true?" their dad asked over dinner that night. He took his napkin from his lap and wiped his mouth.

"I think Miss Baden definitely saw it," Tiffany said. "I don't think she'd make it up."

"But do you think it was Joe Baldwin?" their mom asked. She raised her eyebrows over her glass of water and cut her eyes back and forth between Pearl and Tiffany.

The twins looked at one another, each one afraid to say what they thought, either for fear of making the legend true or ruining it altogether.

That night, after they were both in bed and the house was dark, Pearl took her walkie-talkie from under her pillow and radioed her sister. "You asleep?" she asked. She waited a moment, the low buzz of static the only sound in the house.

"No," Tiffany radioed back. "What are you doing?"

"Thinking about Joe Baldwin," Pearl said.

"Me too," Tiffany said. "What's on your mind?"

"I think we should go to Maco," Pearl said.

"I think so too," Tiffany said. "Tomorrow's Friday. Let's ask Dad."

The next morning, amidst the chaos of eating breakfast, dressing for school, finding homework and packed lunches and water bottles and backpacks, the twins pitched their dad on their plan. They'd opened the family laptop and done their research while eating cereal that morning.

"It gets dark at 6:15 tonight," Pearl said.

"And it's only an hour to Maco," Tiffany added.

"We can be there and back by nine o'clock easily," Pearl said. Their bedtime was 9:30 p.m. on the weekends, and the twins knew this sign of maturity would appeal to their dad.

"Please," Tiffany said.

"Please," Pearl echoed.

Their dad sighed. He picked up his car keys and shooed them out the front door. "Okay, okay," he said.

"Yes!" the twins said at the same time.

"Just don't let it go to your *heads*."

The girls both groaned, but the dad jokes hadn't stopped there. Even now, cruising down the highway to investigate the Maco Light for themselves, their dad was still at it. He continued tapping his ring against the steering wheel, now to the beat of Taylor Swift's "I Knew You Were Trouble" while it played on the radio. As soon as the song ended he looked in the rearview mirror and found his daughters' eyes. "I've always liked Taylor Swift," he said. "She seems to have a good *head* on her shoulders."

"Please stop," Tiffany said.

"What?" their dad said. "What did I say?"

Pearl leafed through photocopies she'd made that day in the North Carolina Room at the public library downtown. Their teacher, Mrs. Todd, had taken the class on a field trip, and they'd spent the morning in the history room, researching the various stories the students had been assigned. Tiffany had a stack of photocopies on her lap as well. The light had faded too much to read, so Pearl clicked on the back seat's dome light. "Look at this," she said, handing a paper to her sister.

Tiffany read in silence for a moment, and then she looked up. "This says that Joe Baldwin was hoping to get back to Hamlet that night so he could ask his girlfriend Savannah to marry him."

"Where's Hamlet?" Pearl asked.

"It's a couple hours west," their dad said. "The town essentially exists because of the railroad."

"I guess Joe Baldwin never made it back to her," Tiffany said.

"Poor Savannah," Pearl said.

Their dad sighed in the front seat. "I bet she hung her *head* and cried," he said.

Both girls groaned.

An hour later their father had crossed the median and pulled into a little turnout off the side of the highway, parking the car east toward Wilmington. It was full dark now, and the only sounds were the occasional swishing of tires over the wet asphalt as cars and trucks whipped past, gently rocking the car where it sat. Their father turned around in his seat and faced them. "Are y'all ready to investigate?" he asked.

The twins looked at one another and nodded, doing their best to smile despite their growing apprehension.

Suddenly a light cut through the darkness, and a flashlight's beam shone on their father's face from below. "No matter what," he said, his voice dropping an octave, "don't lose your *heads*."

"No wonder Mom didn't come," Tiffany said.

"Some people don't like scary stuff," their dad said, clicking off the flashlight.

"The only thing scary out here is your sense of humor," said Pearl.

But that wasn't quite true. It was dark out there, darker than either Pearl or Tiffany could have imagined. Although all of them had flashlights, the twins followed the beam of their father's light as he led them away from the car, down a gravel road, and into the woods along what seemed to have once been a railroad corridor. They stood in the middle of what felt like a tunnel in the woods, the ground clear and open beneath them and for ten feet on either side, the boughs of the pine trees all around them nearly touching above, a canopy so thick it would've blocked out the moonlight had there been a moon out that night.

"This is your investigation," their dad said. "Lead the way."

For the next hour, Pearl and Tiffany walked up and down the corridor, probably a half mile in either direction. It was clear that a railroad had once run beneath their feet—they even discovered some old wooden ties piled atop one another in the woods at one point—but there was no sign of Joe Baldwin, the blue light of his lantern, or the head he'd supposedly spent every night since the accident searching for.

Slowly, their hopes began to dwindle, and their moods slid from cautious adventure to disappointed resignation. After what felt like hours, Pearl was the first to throw in the towel. "I think we should go home," she said.

"I think so too," added Tiffany, as if she'd been waiting for Pearl to make the call.

"Are you sure?" their dad asked. "Are you really ready to *head* back to Wilmington?"

It was getting late, and the twins were tired, too tired even to acknowledge the bad joke.

"Poor Savannah," their dad said in a clear attempt to lift his daughters' moods. "It looks like ol' Joe ain't gonna make it to Hamlet tonight."

But everything changed when they got back to the car. The twins were strapped in and settled into the back seat by the time they realized their dad couldn't get the engine going. At first they thought he was kidding, an extension of the jokes he'd been making for days.

"Come on, Dad," Tiffany said, "be serious."

"Yeah," Pearl said. "Be serious."

But their dad didn't say anything. He just continued to turn the key in the ignition, and the car continued not to respond. "I guess the battery's dead," he said. The twins heard the sound of the hood latch popping free, and they watched from the back seat as their dad climbed out of the car, opened the hood, and stood peering down at the engine. They knew their dad understood little about cars, and they knew that his inspection was cursory, something people did whenever cars didn't work, regardless of whether or not they knew how to fix them. After a few minutes their dad closed the hood and got back behind the wheel. He turned to face them.

"Listen," he said, "we passed a convenience store about a mile back. I'm going to walk down there and ask someone to drive me back with jumper cables to get the battery going."

"What if it's closed?" Tiffany asked.

Their dad looked at his watch. "It's not even nine," he said. "They'll be open."

"We're going with you, right?" Pearl asked.

Their dad sighed. "I think it would be easier and safer if y'all stayed here. I wouldn't feel safe with three of us walking along the highway in the dark." As if proving his point a tractor trailer whipped by them at that moment, rocking the car as if it were a raft on the ocean.

"I don't want to stay here alone," Tiffany said.

Their dad smiled. "You won't be alone, honey. You two will be together." He widened his eyes. "*I'll* be the one who's all alone." He smiled again. "I'll be back in just a few minutes." He fished his cell phone out of his pocket and handed it to Pearl. "Here," he said. "You can watch something while you wait." He narrowed his eyes. "But only cartoons," he said. "I'm serious."

The girls nodded, and then he opened the door and stepped out into the night. The twins were quiet for a moment until Pearl unlocked the screen on their dad's phone and opened the Netflix app. "What do you want to watch?" she asked.

"I don't care," Pearl said. "Definitely nothing scary."

Pearl stared at the phone in her hand, waiting. The circle on the app that signified the download spun interminably. "It's not working," she said. She closed the app and opened it again, but the result was the same. She clicked the screen to black and tossed it on the seat between them.

Tiffany checked to make sure her door was locked, and then

she reached across Pearl to check her door as well. She sat for a moment, and then she leaned into the front seat and did the same.

"Paranoid much?" Pearl asked.

"Don't start," Tiffany said. "This was your idea."

"No, it wasn't," Pearl said.

"Yes, it was."

"I'm calling Mom," Pearl said.

"Fine," Tiffany said. "She's going to kill Dad for leaving us alone."

Pearl stared at the phone for a moment, and then she picked it up and dialed their mom's number. She waited for it to ring, but nothing happened. "So weird," she said.

"Yeah," Tiffany said. "This whole night has been weird."

They sat without talking, easing closer and closer to one another across the seat until their legs were touching. They rested their heads against the backs of their seats, and soon they were asleep.

Even in sleep, Pearl was aware of her sister's presence on the seat beside her, and she dreamed that they were nestled beneath a roof made of a sheet spread across four chairs they had used in constructing a pillow fort in the living room back home. They were spending the night inside the fort, and they were both fast asleep, and that was why Pearl couldn't understand why the movie they'd fallen asleep watching was so bright on the other side of her closed eyes.

On the seat beside her, Tiffany dreamt of being in a kayak with Pearl and their dad. Perhaps they were paddling home from Shark Tooth Island. Tiffany could feel the waves lapping beneath the boat, and from the helm she sensed her sister's presence behind her, her dad's presence at the rear of the boat. Tiffany could feel the paddle in her hands, and she was striking at the water wildly, trying to move the kayak away from the bright blue light of what must be a boat bearing down on them.

The sisters woke up in the back seat at the same moment, both of them blinded by the blue light barreling toward their car. Although it was silent, the light moved with the speed of a locomotive. They screamed, closed their eyes, held their arms over their faces in attempts to block the light. But it was impossible not to see it, and it was impossible not to feel it as it moved through the windshield, into the car, across their bodies, and into the darkness behind them.

Just like that, it was gone. Both girls turned in their seats and looked out the back of the car to see where the light had gone, but it had disappeared. They opened their mouths to say something, perhaps to ask where the light had gone or if it had even been real, but a sound outside the car stopped them from speaking.

It was the sound of the hood creaking open. Someone was at work on the engine.

"Dad?!" Pearl called out, but no one answered. The only sounds they could hear were coming from the other side of the open hood.

Tiffany slid even closer to her sister. "Call Mom again," she said.

"The phone doesn't work," Pearl said.

"Just try."

Pearl looked around and found that the phone had fallen onto the floorboard. When she picked it up the screen came alive, revealing that it was after 2:30 a.m. How was that possible? How had so much time passed? She punched in her dad's code, called their mom, but again, nothing.

They both jumped at the sound of the hood slamming shut. Their father opened the driver's side door and slid in behind the steering wheel. He brought with him the damp smell of night: cold rain and wet leaves and clothing. The girls both sighed in relief upon seeing him return, and their spirits lifted when he turned the key and the engine roared to life. They were going home.

"How long were you gone?" Pearl asked. Their father shrugged his shoulders.

"How did you fix the car by yourself?" Tiffany asked. "I thought you were coming back with someone. I though you needed jumper cables."

There was only silence from the front seat.

Their father pulled onto the highway headed east back toward Wilmington. The car was silent, the radio now off. Pearl looked at her dad's hands on the steering wheel, noticed that he was missing his wedding ring. She opened her mouth to ask if he'd lost it, but then she saw his hands: the long fingers she'd never noticed before, the veins that ridged the backs of his hands. His hands were filthy, smeared with grease and dirt. "Dad?" she said. "Dad? Where's your ring?"

The car slowed, and their dad put on his blinker and merged into the left lane toward a break in the median. He turned the car around so that they were now headed west.

"Where are we going?" Tiffany asked.

"Dad?" Pearl said.

They passed a sign showing that Hamlet was 107 miles away.

"Where are we going?" Tiffany asked again.

Their father turned in his seat and looked at them for a moment. His eyes were deep black pits. He tried to smile as if to comfort them, but they'd never seen his face take on such a look before. A thin black line ran diagonally across his neck as if he were wearing a tight necklace. A single drop of blood beaded around it. He faced the road again.

"Dad?" Tiffany said. "What's going on?" She leaned forward and touched his shoulder. It was stiff, the black jacket he was wearing—had he been wearing it when they left home?—was cold and hard.

She pulled her hand back and looked at her sister. There were tears in Pearl's eyes. Something was wrong. Then their father spoke. His voice came from deep in his chest, like a bottomless cavern had opened to allow a ghostly wind to escape.

"I'm going to Hamlet," their father said. "Savannah's been waiting."

Gravity Hill

—SYNORA HUNT CUMMINGS—

Seventeen. That's how old she was the night she met J.D. Lightning bugs synchronized against the opaque darkness in the humid night. Beneath the front porch light hung a swag of pure white roses, and the screen door spring creaked with each open and shut, its rusty cry announcing the arrival of family and friends who had come to feed the mourning and pay their last respects. Mrs. Berniece left a legacy of hot biscuits and coffee, summer vegetables from the deep freezer for anyone in need, and sacred advice steeped in the King James Version. Folks were gathering from near and far to sit up with the dead, each with a recollection of the impact Mrs. Berniece had left, stories of how she and Grandpa Horace raised nine head o' young'uns on nothing but love and hard work. They'd done well for themselves, and it was evident through the accomplishments of their offspring.

Them young'uns went on to be somebody and never had to farm another day in their lives. Now that Marge Ann, she was something else. She topped them all. She was beauty and brains. Marge Ann went up the road for her schooling and made a real fine life for herself. She married that boy of Preacher Grant's. He finished up at the community college while he waited for Marge Ann to come home. That gal never did make it back, so he followed her. Made a mighty fine electrician of himself. Well known. Started his own business and got people working for him all over the state of Georgia. Marge Ann works government contract. She could work from anywhere in the world. Once she started having them babies, she started coming home in the summers. Her and Berniece would tend that garden. When her gals got old enough, they tended too. That oldest one is the spitting image of her momma, just as smart as Marge Ann ever dared to be. Marge Ann's got 'em in the kitchen now. She won't let 'em sit down. Berniece was the same way with her crowd. She was always so proud of her young'uns and made sure they knew the right way.

Myra had made her way out of the kitchen. She needed a break from the chatter and the questions of what she planned to do after high school. The crowd was a bit overwhelming, but she reveled in the presence of all who knew and loved her grandmother so well. She could only hope to be a pillar of strength and resilience as Grandma Berniece had been. Little cousins were playing hide-and-seek, running tirelessly, brushing back sweat-streaked hair. Older cousins had retreated to the screened back porch beneath a dim light and ceiling fan, and Myra made her way there. Grandma Berniece had made sure there was plenty of seating for Sunday afternoon gatherings. Myra escaped to the old tire swing hung by rusty galvanized rope from the grand oak tree that had stood at the end of that old dirt road for nearly a century. Myra emptied the collected rainwater from the tire; she didn't mind so much if her black eyelet dress got a little wet. This was her favorite pastime. She closed her eyes as she gently pushed herself off with her feet. Though the air was thick, she liked the way it wisped through her auburn-brown ringlets. She could almost feel Grandpa Horace's hands giving her a push as Grandma Berniece yelled from the porch in her half apron, "Horace, you be easy with them young'uns now!" Though she had not been born in North Carolina, this is where she felt deeply rooted. She believed that no matter how successful she would ever become, she would always come back to the place that shaped her.

"Hey, mind if I give you a push?" Myra was startled by the deep voice coming from the person who had quietly made his way across the yard. With a slight jolt of her heart, she opened her eyes. "I'm sorry. I didn't mean to scare you. You're Myra, right?" She gave a slight sheepish nod. "I'm J.D. Your grandpa Horace taught my dad's Sunday School class when he was a young boy." J.D. was two years her senior. He was tall and built lean and hard. His hazel eyes popped against his caramel skin and coal-black hair. Enamored by his beauty, she eased herself from the swing and wiped her sweaty palms against the bodice of her dress. "Hey. Yes. My grandpa always enjoyed doing anything at church."

J.D.'s family hadn't attended the same church in many years, but that never hindered an occasional visit for Sunday lunch at Horace and Berniece's home place. Friends, new and old, were warmly welcomed at that long maple wood table that seated eight, built by Grandpa Horace himself. Diners took shifts at the table while overflow settled on the porches or at TV trays in the living room. J.D. always found solace at this end of the dirt road. There were cornfields to the left and a cattail-lined canal to the right beyond the packhouse. Berniece kept her flower beds and potted plants as meticulously as her garden. Horace was always keeping up with repairs on the old, weathered plank board house. There was always something pulling J.D. to this place that he couldn't quite explain until this moment beneath the canopy that symbolized all that Horace and Berniece were rooted in.

Myra's little sister Madelynn stood off in the distance near the end of the porch and threw one hand on her hip. "Myra Jane, Momma is lookin' you. She said the sweet tea is 'bout gone and she needs you to make some more. She said to get Grandma's pickle jar out of the pantry to make another gallon." J.D. gave a slight drop of his head as he pushed his hands into his pockets.

"I'm sorry, I guess I better head back in," Myra said softly. J.D. gently nudged the tire swing with his foot and hung back until Myra had completed the seemingly long journey back to the kitchen. Myra's mind reeled. Why had she never met J.D. before? How much time had he spent with her grandparents? She needed to know more about him.

Back in the kitchen, Marge Ann was cutting pound cake into slices. The aunties were tidying up what visitors had left behind. The church ladies had taken a break to sit around the table, reminiscing and prophesying with the last of Horace's and Berniece's siblings. Maggie, the second oldest of Marge Ann's children, had put the kettle on to steep the tea. Myra retrieved the gallon pickle jar from the pantry lined with seasonal vegetables and jams that she had helped her grandmother put up summer after summer. She noticed a jar of honey from the Bent Tree Bee Farm sitting among the green beans. She rehomed it to its proper place among the syrups and molasses kept for those warm fluffy biscuits and grabbed the tub of sugar on her way out.

"Momma, I've never made tea in this jar before. How many cups of sugar?" Berniece had a special coffee cup that she used to measure just the right amount of sugar, Maggie had pulled it from the cabinet. "Oh, do one full cup and a little less than half. That oughta do it. I never did like it as sweet as momma did." The girls giggled, because surely Myra would now do two full cups just the way Grandma would have told her to do. When the tea had steeped just long enough, Maggie poured it over the sugar while Myra stirred with a wooden spoon. Then they steeped a second kettle.

"Well, Myra and Maggie, I don't believe I've seen you two since you were tiny little ol' thangs. Y'all have grown into some beautiful young ladies. Myra, I hear you're headed off to college here soon. Where you planning on going, shug? My J.D. just finished up his first year at Pembroke State. He never was one to go far from home." Myra was flooded with the information her brain had just taken in. Mrs. Rose was sitting among the church ladies reminiscing and prophesying. She had heard Grandma Berniece speak of her on several occasions to say, "That boy o' Roses's is coming by tomorrow to help Horace cut corn," or anything else of the sort that Grandpa Horace needed help with.

"My plans are to attend Georgia Tech to study biomedical engineering," Myra said with confidence.

"Well, that's all right. Sounds like you might have something in common with my oldest boy, J.D. He hopes to become a physician's assistant someday," Rose said with great pride in her voice. Myra gave a glance across the kitchen to see that J.D. was now in the living room waiting patiently for his family. He spoke gingerly and respectfully with the elders. His demeanor was soft and calm, a gentleness she'd observed in the most revered men in her life. Somehow she knew everything she needed to know.

Thirteen years had passed since the day Myra and J.D. tied the knot. It had been a beautiful crisp autumn day beneath that grand oak tree at the end of the dirt road. Nothing had given Preacher Grant more delight than officiating his oldest granddaughter in marriage to J.D. in the presence of God, family, and the community he cherished. It was a small and meaningful wedding celebrating the legacy that had been lived before each of them. And through the years that old plank board house at the end of the dirt road provided the backdrop and represented the very foundation J.D. and Myra would continue building their life upon. It had become their home—a place where laughter echoed through the halls, where the scent of biscuits and sweet tea lingered in the air, and where the garden bloomed each spring with Berniece's roses. Over the years, they had restored the house with care, preserving its soul while adding touches of their own: a nursery painted in soft yellow, a porch swing J.D. built by hand, and an upgraded kitchen where Myra would teach their daughter, Mercy, the same recipes passed down through generations. It was more than a house—it was a living memory, a sacred place where loved endured, even after death.

That night there was a chill in the air, and Myra had taken notice of the hoot owl off in the distance as she settled Mercy into the car. A dense fog had settled between the towering pines and lingered over the murky swamps along those winding country roads. There wasn't a star in sight, but the moon hung low and bright, casting a cold and watchful eye over the eerie black canvas.

J.D. loaded up the diaper bag into the back seat and slammed the door shut. Myra was waiting in the passenger seat hugging herself closely to retain as much body heat as possible. J.D. jumped into the driver's seat, gave the key a turn, and pumped the gas pedal. The old Chevy gave a bit of a choke before finally sputtering to a start. J.D. slapped the dashboard appreciatively and exclaimed, "Atta girl, ol' Bessie, you get us on home now. I got two fine ladies to take care of." Myra grinned slyly with the click of her seatbelt. She took in a deep breath filling her lungs with gratitude for the time her little family had shared with her parents and sisters and their families.

As they pulled away, the headlights cut through the thick fog that had settled low over the fields. The road to home twisted like a ribbon through the pines, their silhouettes looming like silent sentinels. As they neared the stop sign at the bottom of the hill just before the long dirt road, Myra glanced to the right and caught a glimpse of a porch light flickering—once, twice—before going dark. A chill ran down her spine. She turned forward again, trying to shake the feeling that something was watching them from the tree line. The baby stirred in the back seat, letting out a soft whimper just as the radio crackled to life, unprompted, untouched, whispering a faint gospel tune. J.D. reached to adjust the dial, but the static only grew louder. "Must be the fog," he muttered, but Myra wasn't so sure. Ol' Bessie stalled out. J.D. kept his foot on the brake as the car rolled just past the stop sign and into the intersection. Myra stared out into the night, her heart beginning to race, as the Chevy came to a slow stop.

As J.D. threw his door open and stepped into the night, he waved Myra back, motioning for her to stay inside. "I'll push. You just keep it in neutral," he said calmly over his shoulder. Myra hesitated as she reached over and her fingers tightened over the steering wheel. The baby was now fully awake and fussing. J.D. braced himself against the front of Ol' Bessie, his boots slipping slightly on the damp gravel as he began to push. The car inched up the hill, tires slowly crunching. Then, from the left, a pair of headlights burst through the fog—too fast, too close. Myra let out a frantic scream. J.D. turned just in time to see the blur before he was struck with a sickening thud that hurled him into the ditch. The gospel tune on the radio was replaced by a deafening silence that filled Myra's ears. J.D. lay crumpled and helpless in the ditch, his body contorted unnaturally against the ditch lilies. Blood trickled from a gash across his brow, pooling in the mud beneath him. His right leg was bent at an unimaginable angle, snapped like a branch. His arm lay limp, shattered from the impact. His breaths came shallow and ragged, each one a struggle. The night's fog furled around him and swallowed Myra's screams as she threw the car in park and stumbled out, her heart pounding in her throat. The dimming headlights barely reached J.D., but she could see his still and broken body. She dropped to her knees, her hands trembling as she touched his face. "J.D., please,

please stay with me," she whispered as she brushed his blood-soaked hair from his forehead. His eyes fluttered, and he let out a faint groan. Myra fumbled for her phone, her hands shaking so desperately she nearly dropped it. No signal. The baby's cries were now rising to a fever pitch. This night—it all felt like a trap closing in. She looked back at the vehicle. Panic clawed at her chest. She needed to move, but her legs felt rooted in the ditch. She was torn between the man she loved as he bled beside her and the child screaming in the back seat. Every breath felt like a weight. She forced herself to stand, swaying with nausea, and staggered to the car. She yanked the car door open and reached into the back seat, her hands slick with J.D.'s blood. "Shh, it's okay. I've got you," she whispered as she clutched the baby to her chest. Mercy's warmth anchored her in the chaos.

She looked back at J.D.'s motionless body in the ditch, and her heart twisted. She needed help. She couldn't leave J.D., but she couldn't risk the baby either. She made a decision. She would drive to the nearest house, call an ambulance, then come back. With one last glance at the love of her life, she whispered, "Hold on, please. I'm coming back."

With Myra and the baby gone, the fog continued to thicken around J.D.'s broken body. He lay motionless in the ditch, his breath shallow and uneven. Minutes passed. Maybe longer. Time unraveled in slow, uneven threads.

A soft, unhurried movement rustled in the grass. J.D.'s fingers twitched. Somewhere deep in his consciousness, agony bloomed deep in his chest. His eyes fluttered open, unfocused. He tried to speak, but his throat was dry and raspy. He could feel the fog seeping into his bones.

And then he heard it.

A voice. A low whisper. It wasn't a voice he recognized. It wasn't his beloved Myra's. It was low and melodic. It came from the trees, or maybe it was from the fog itself. His eyes widened, his body was too battered to move.

The whisper grew louder.

And then it stopped.

Stillness settled over J.D., loud and suffocating. He lifted his gaze upward toward the canopy of pines, and for a moment he thought he saw something standing at the edge of the ditch. Not moving. Not talking. Just watching.

Then he closed his eyes and the light took him.

It was nearly ten o'clock at night when Myra returned to the old homeplace for the first time since J.D.'s passing. The house had stood empty for nearly seven years, but the garden still bloomed ferociously with Berniece's roses, and the grand oak tree still stretched its limbs far and wide over the land. Myra had come to say goodbye, to finally let go of the place that had shaped her and the man she had loved so deeply.

She stopped the car at the stop sign at the bottom of the hill just before the dirt road. The baby, now a seven-year-old with wide hazel eyes, sat quietly in the back seat clutching her favorite stuffed elephant. "Momma," she whispered gingerly, "why are you just sitting here?"

"I just want to see something," Myra replied with a longing in her voice. She cut the engine and waited. For a few seconds there was only silence, then the radio crackled and the faint strains of a gospel hymn filtered through static. The car began to move slow and steady up the hill. Myra's heart beat franticly in her chest.

Mercy clutched her elephant, "Momma, I see someone in white standing at the ditch." Myra's hands trembled as she reached for the ignition, but then she saw them.

Handprints.

Handprints pressed into the dust on the hood of the car. J.D.'s handprints.

Tears filled Myra's eyes from the overwhelming love that lingered in the air. J.D. was still watching over them. Still pushing them to safety.

As the car crested the hill and the engine stammered back to life, Myra whispered, "Thank you, J.D."

My Family Arrives at the Beach

—JULIE FUNDERBURK—

On cold sand, we want ghosts, the coast
full of desires so strong they can't leave.
New yet familiar, the salt air and waves—
memory is rejoining the physical. We know this place.
Crabs scuttle across our beams.
The Gray Ghost who is faceless
warns of storms and wants us gone. Love is often death's
undisputed cause, as with The Bride
who hunts the ring her elder brother flung to the sea.
She's a figment veil, the caps beneath the moon.
Our father who is telling these stories
lets her voice wail: "I want my *ring*. Give me my *ring*."
He is tall to us and happy at the start
of a long-deserved trip. He knows how to shape
vacated destiny. He leads us toward a lit pier
miles distant, insisting that the ring will wash up there.
We can't get that far. But its thwarted promise,
a circle unlived, is a diamond we believe in.
If it takes years, we'll wait the years it takes him
to show us, our father who whispers
in ears. On the dark beach, we laugh as he taps
us on the back, his moaning making us scream.

from The Door That Always Opens, *LSU Press, 2016*

A House of Vine and Shadow

PART TWO — LONGLEAF

"Do you think he needs to hear more?" the old man said.

"Look at his face."

"I think he needs to hear more."

"The last few needed more."

"The last several."

"And some of 'em still didn't understand."

"Some to most, I'd say."

"You'd say right, then."

"You see," the old man said, and he leaned toward Nate, and though he came no closer than the few inches gained by his new angle, when he next spoke Nate could feel the old man's breath in his ear, "some hear such as we're telling you, and seek to prove or disprove by science, by evidence and measurement."

"Foot," the old woman spat.

"Others hear such not as stories but as—what's the word?—curiosities, or artifacts."

"Relics!" the old woman cried. "Shipwrecks and ruins! Nothing more!"

"Little mementos of what an ignorant lot we were, some of us, and some of us still are."

"Not like them now, in their big cities, watching their TVs and talking on their telephones and cooking on their fancy electric stoves."

"What?" was not the question Nate wanted to ask, but it was all he could get out.

"We get a spate of y'all every time the state makes a big jump, finds itself flush with cash, gets a bit above its raising," the old man said as if to soothe him, and though he did not rise or cross the room or reach out Nate felt a hand pat his knee.

"Y'all are the sort to worry about the place not being what it once was, and so its people not being who they once were," the old woman said. "Y'all are the sort to notice the quiet little things you're losing amid all the big, loud, shiny things you're getting."

"As if the one or the other held all the good or the bad."

"So you take hold of some of these stories..."

"Or college basketball."

"Or racing stock cars or eating barbecue or cooking in cast iron and you make sure you misunderstand 'em..."

"Make 'em carry more than they was ever meant to."

"Pin 'em like butterflies behind a glass case."

"I don't," Nate spurted. "I don't think I am who y'all seem to think I am."

"You are," the old woman said, smiling kindly.

"I'm Nate Batts with the Goldleaf Company, and I'm here to make an offer more than fair..."

"Oh, we know," the old man said.

"We heard you the first time."

"The thing is, son, you need to hear these stories, and you need to try to really hear them."

"You need these stories. You needed them long since."

"So maybe the thing is to hear some more."

"Maybe you'll be the one to understand."

Nate sputtered some vowel sounds and tried to shake his head to clear it but found his head could hardly move. He felt like he was swimming against a strong current, swimming upriver against fast and shallow water. The old man smiled and opened his mouth and inhaled to begin to speak, but somehow when he drew breath, Nate could feel a light wind against his cheek, and on that wind he could smell a bright scent that made him remember his grandmother mopping her kitchen floor.

The old man caught whatever he'd been about to say, and said instead, "That there's the longleaf pine."

Then he began.

Ol' Jack Spooks the Devil

—ED SOUTHERN—

Come a morning Mahaliel Hide, like every firstborn Hide man before him, took a ride around the land he pretended was his. Mah rode not on a horse but an Indian Scout Sixty, near-giddy still at the *vroom vroom vroom* of the four-stroke engine, even after all such mornings, even after all his years, and since the Hides once held claim to quite a bit of land in Comeknock County, he could get a lot of *vroom* come a morning.

They'd owned most all of the gentle slope where old-town, downtown Hidetown sat. They'd owned good bottomland along two of Comeknock County's three big creeks, Muddy, Bloody, and Mill. They'd owned tracts along the Trading Ford Road that climbed west out of Hidetown to follow the brown Donnoha River, too thick to drink and too thin to plow, up into the Moratock Mountains. Through their bank they'd owned a goodly piece of the Greengrass Mines that dug copper out of those mountains. They'd owned the furniture factory on the Donnoha's banks at the Moratocks' foot. They'd owned most of the big forest called Surewood, out of whose never-ending timbers they made that furniture.

And there in the Surewood forest they'd owned the single poorest piece of land in all of Comeknock, if not the state, if not the world. It lay at the end of a thin red-clay trickle of a trail that once had been part of the Great Trading Path, off a little gravelly spur that once had been part of the Great Wagon Road, off the Charlotte Highway that ran south out of Hidetown. It lay at the geographic center of the state, at the intersection of one line that ran from the bootheel of Andrew Jackson's statue in New Orleans to General Lee's lower lip on Stone Mountain on to Kings Mountain and Capitol Hill and Independence Hall and L'Anse aux Meadows, and another line that ran from the Lost City of Z through the Bermuda Triangle to the spot where the Witch of November took the *Edmund Fitzgerald.* At this crossing lay a circle of perfect chords and ratio, inside of which nothing grew. The soil of this circle, should you somehow find some on your tongue, tasted like ashes and salt.

What you'd really be tasting, though, was brimstone and sulfur.

This is how it was, you see: When Mah Hide's distant ancestor Malachiliel Hide first came to Comeknock County, he came a rich man. He came with men who obeyed him, some by choice and some not. He came with a wagon full of sacks of seed, a herd of swine and a flock of hens, and a cow named Nellie of which he was most proud. Nellie gave the sweetest-tasting milk anyone Mal Hide had yet met had ever tasted, and Mal Hide was most proud of that, not that he had anything to do with it. Long lines of bulls and heifers had come together to produce this sweet-milk-giving Nellie; Mal Hide just happened to have come into possession of her. Still, he was proud, of his good fortune, I guess. Not that he had anything to do with that, either.

Anyway, he came from Virginia with Pennsylvania-made furniture and bolts of fabric and two things that no man had ever seen before in that part of the world: a title and a deed.

The land that would become Comeknock County was then

full of outlaws and rogues and others of whom polite society had run afoul, who would not or could not be expected to honor a title and a deed. They would or could be expected to snatch them from the bearer's fingers and use them to wipe their—if the former bearer was lucky—noses. But old Mal Hide had a stout and a bold heart. He had a sword and a brace of pistols on his belt. He had a steady hand and an unwavering eye and an unshakable confidence in his ability to make a mutually profitable deal with even the vilest blackguard the land had to offer.

So Malachiliel Hide came riding into what would come to be called Comeknock County on a fine black stallion and proceeded to ride the length and breadth of the land to which he held title and deed. He came to the foot of the first of the Moratock Mountains and showed his men where he wanted his house built. He rode along the creeks and the bank of the Donnoha River. He rode through the Surewood Forest, and he happened upon the single poorest piece of land in what would be Comeknock County. And there he met the first soul he had encountered since he'd entered what would be Comeknock County.

And that just happened to be Jack.

I shouldn't say "just happened to be," because that says that Jack's being in the midst of that salt-and-ashes circle was purely coincidence, and it wasn't. Old Mal Hide would not have met any other future Comeknocker in the midst of that circle. Only Jack would have been there, and could have been there, and I'm about to tell you why.

Mal Hide said, "Good morrow, sirrah," or whatever it was olden times people said when they wanted to say good morning.

Jack said back, "Good morning," except he said it in an old-timey way too, of course.

Mal Hide tells him, "I am the owner of this land. I have title and deed, and now I come in body to lay claim and to settle. I will not have you prosecuted for trespass. In fact, I will let you stay on this land and work as my tenant."

Jack said, "No, that's all right. I can move along now, once you pay me my wages for the labor I performed you last night."

Mal Hide could see that Jack looked hollow-eyed and short of breath, that Jack's hair was slicked down with sweat and Jack's cheeks were flushed a deep red. He had put that to carousing rather than labor, though. He asked Jack what labor he had performed and how it was of benefit to him, who had only arrived that morning.

Jack said, "I cleared the Devil off this land."

Mal Hide smiled the kind of smile you smile to idiots and crazy people.

Jack said, "I didn't even mean to. Had I set out to contend with the Devil I'd have been guilty of the sin of pride, and that's one sin I ain't guilty of. I just come along by accident and the Devil took to contending with me."

"Oh, Lord, forgive me," Jack said. "To say the Devil took to contending with me makes me sound all puffed-up and important, because to *con-tend* means to struggle with an opponent who is more or less your equal, and for me to hold myself equal in power to the Devil would make me guilty of the sin of pride, and . . ."

"And that's one you ain't guilty of," Mal Hide said. "I got that part. It's the particulars, the plotline, so to speak, that I lack."

Jack said, "Right you are. I was walking to my sleeping place last night, and I must've got lost in the forest. For next thing I see is Old Scratch himself, tramping round and round this circle, his hooves burning the ground with each step. I turned to run, but the Devil he says, 'Come back here,' and I was so scared that I did. He said he needed to ask me something. He said all he needed was information and that I had nothing to fear since he was too vexed to tempt my soul away.

"I was wary, and knew better than to credit what he said, but I told him to ask his question and I'd answer him as best I could.

"He fixed me with his awful eyes and he says, 'What the hell is it with you people around here?'

"I said, 'Pardon me?'

"He said, 'Boy, are you asking the wrong guy for that. I'll ask you again, What the hell is it with you people around here?'

"I said, 'Sir, I don't know that I know what you mean.'

"He said, 'This here's been my favorite pondering spot for I don't know how long. Good views, nice breezes, and a real cool, kind of off-kilter feel to it. Kind of a Jonestown vibe, know what I mean? No, wait, you don't know what I mean, hasn't happened yet. Being eternal can be such a bitch when it comes to conversations. Point being, I like it here.'

"'Then you people started moving in, and the place started going downhill fast. I mean, the Peoples had sense enough to keep their distance. But you white folks'll throw up your little cabins anywhere. I'll just come out and say it, you people spook me. What the hell is up with that?'

"I said, 'Well, people need land, I guess,' but he shushed me and said, 'Oh, Jesus, don't you go telling me what people need, or what they want, neither. I know more about that than just about anybody. That's like telling a snake how to bite. Come to think of it, that *is* telling a snake how to bite. Heh heh.'

"'I know that people need land. You got any idea what the soul-to-land exchange rate on this continent is right now? I'm cleaning up. I'm raking y'all in hand over fist. You wouldn't believe what kind of nonsense you people will do for land. Sometimes, even *I* can't believe what y'all'll do. And when someone makes me say, *Whoa*, then buddy, they have hit the degeneracy jackpot.'

"I shrugged and said, 'Well, I guess that's your answer, then.'

"The Devil said, 'No, no, no, that's the problem. You people around here, you'd think you'd be easy to tempt. Nothing but a bunch of misfits and losers who can't seem to hack it in civilization. Always got a jug of moonshine and a pipe in your hands. But it's like you people have some kind of force field around you, you know? Wait, you don't know what a force field is, do you? Stupid eternality.'

"'Put it this way—it's like you're too damn stupid for me to tempt. I ran into a couple of jokers last week who asked me if I wanted to drink and play cards with them. Who the hell wants to play cards with the Devil?

"'Let's take you,' he said. 'What's your name?'

"I said I'd just as soon not tell him.

"He said, 'Dadgummit, Jack, I already know your name. I was just giving you a chance to be polite. Anyway, tell me what you want.'

"I said I'd really like to be going on to my sleeping place right now.

"He said, 'Yeah, yeah, that much is obvious. But what do you really want? Wait a minute—you said your sleeping place? Ain't you got no house to go to?'

"I said no.

"He said, 'Nor a bed to lay down on?'

"I said no.

"He said, 'You want a big house with a fine feather bed?'

"I pondered on it and said, 'No, I like my sleeping place.'

"He said, 'Do what? Damn. Well, what do you want then? What does your heart desire? Tell me and it'll be yours.'

"I pondered on it, and I told him, honestly, that I couldn't think of anything.

"He said, 'What do you mean you can't think of anything? You want riches?'

"I said I wouldn't have a place to put it.

"He said I could buy a place to put it.

"I said, 'But then I'd not have as many riches.'

"He said he'd throw in a place to put my riches.

"I said, 'But then I'd have all the trouble of keeping that place tidy and presentable.'

"He said he'd throw in a servant to keep the place tidy.

"I said, 'But then I'd have to pay the servant and I'd not have as many riches.'

"He said, 'But you'd have plenty more riches.'

"I said, 'Yeah, but from what I hear, once you get riches all you want is more riches, and if you got to give some of your riches to pay a servant then you got to go to the trouble of making more riches to get back what you've lost, and that's too much trouble for me.'

"He said, 'All right, then, how about a woman? You want the most beautiful woman in the world?'

"I said, 'There is a real pretty girl that lives across Muddy Creek.'

"He said, 'I'll get her for you.'

"I said, 'No, don't do that. I've no place fit for a pretty girl to live.'

"He said, 'I'll throw in a place where you both could live.'

"I said, 'No, don't do that. I wouldn't feel right if you got her for me instead of me getting her myself. I couldn't look her in the eye, and what's the point of a pretty girl if you can't look her in the eye? How would I know she'd really love me and not run off with some handsome stranger?'

"He said, 'You want all the food you could ever eat?'

"I said, 'I got all the food I could ever eat. I'm kind of scrawny, if you hadn't noticed.'

"He said, 'You'd grow stout if you had more food.'

"I said, 'Then I'd just need more food.'

"He said, 'But you'd have all the food you could eat. That's the point.'

"I said, 'Yeah, but all the food I can eat now isn't all that much, and all the food I could eat then would be a far sight more. Plus it'd be more of a strain for me to go get it. So no thank you.'

"He said, 'You want to be the king?'

"I said, 'No, hats make my head itch, so I reckon a crown would burn like fire.'

"He said, 'You want the sun to always shine on you?'

"I said, 'No, I'd get sunburnt.'

"He said . . . well, he said a whole bunch of words I'd just as soon not repeat. After he simmered down a bit he looked at me sideways and said, 'You want me to leave you alone?'

"I said, 'Well, to be honest, you ain't bothering me near as much as I expected you would. No offense.'

"He let out a holler then. He stomped his hooves and took to slamming his pitchfork against the ground, cursing every time it struck the soil.

"I said, 'I said, No offense.'

"He settled down and caught his breath and said, 'No, that's all right. I know you didn't mean nothing by it, Jack. It's just that I'm going to have to leave this place, and this has been my favorite pondering spot as long as I can remember. But I can't stay here no more. You people—you people just give me the creeps.'

"And then he up and vanished."

Then, at dawn on the day when I've begun, Mahaliel Hide came riding on his Indian Scout Sixty motorcycle to that salt-and-ashes circle and would've had a start if he hadn't been Mah Hide. For everyone in Comeknock, and a few still in North Carolina, and all in the Old North State, knew this circle to have been the Devil's, his Tromping Grounds, back before the Comeknock's early settlers spooked him and he up and moved to his Tramping Grounds outside Siler City.

Yet on the day when I've begun, just before Mah Hide came upon the barren circle, a body lay sleeping in its center. Nobody went into the Devil's Tromping Grounds, much less lay down inside it, much less went to sleep, much less so close to midsummer. This body, though, belonged to Saint Jack of the Woods, who woke as Mah came riding. Saint Jack raised himself from his belly, shook what dirt he could from his self, and set his cap back straight, the taste of brimstone and sulfur on his tongue. Saint Jack knew those tastes for what they were.

Mah Hide, even though he was Mah Hide, had to blink a few times.

"Morning, Jack," Mah said.

"Morning," Saint Jack said back.

Mah Hide asked him, "What you doing sleeping there, of all places?"

Saint Jack said, "I was here when I give out and couldn't keep going no more."

Mah Hide asked him what he had been doing to wear himself out, and doing right there, of all places.

Saint Jack said, "All I was doing was listening, really, and trying to answer questions as best as I could."

"Who was asking you questions?" Mah Hide asked.

Saint Jack said, "I got to go talk to the preacher."

Mah Hide blinked some more and narrowed his stare at Saint Jack and at the sterile circle. He thought back to the story of his ancestor Mal, a story Mah was among the last to know.

"Who was asking you questions, Jack?"

Saint Jack stretched and rose to his feet and looked all about. "The Devil," he said. "He's done come back."

Break Forth, O Beauteous Heav'nly Light

—ROSS WHITE—

The Little Red Man descends to dig the subbasement of the Single Brothers House.

I have rejoiced in the Bethania summer
festooned with sweet bay magnolia, dogwood, and birch,
a summer decked with creekside doghobble and holly,
a summer sung in the throats of warbler and ovenbird,

and have scoured the brilliant bone-white Salem winter
from hobnail boots, seen the low cannonade of cloud
billow until winter wind marches small mountains of drift
into ranges that glimmer like just-revealed treasure

and I would weather another prismatic summer,
or I would weather another porcelain winter,
but this built Moravia on a hill, this Single Brothers House
is too much autumn. Browning. The first shingles of frost

on the roof of a heart. Too much autumn, the muted
gray of the cornerstones and columns. Too much autumn,
the ochre of footpaths leading to wells in which the dim
depths belch brown water, the ashen oak bark

and leafless limbs, too much autumn, the gardens
with their ambering hedges. The lifeless leather I sew
above a sole, too much autumn. The church. I should wear
a sack, be scratched to red, just to have some color in me again.

Where should I find the tonic for the dour that surrounds
me like a cave? The dingy October heavens offer
little comfort; stoic hymns—*My Redeemer, Overwhelmed*
or *Lord, Who Throughout These Forty Days*—crumble on the
tongue.

There is a world beneath the world. Imagine the reluctant
bend of the earth, the sphere so vast we think it flat,
and then think of our cities risen on the outside
of its arc, our summits and valleys all along its crest.

But were I to dig past water table, through bedrock,
a deeper chamber than ever was torn in the ground,
I might find myself standing above the fine soil
of a Salem from the inner Earth, whose steeples rise

into the depths, whose footpaths bend convex
if you're able to perceive the way they hang
to the underside of that sphere we daily walk atop.
And perhaps its sky is glistening yellow, its stone

a verdant green, its blossoms blue and petals black,
perhaps all its autumns and storms are confined indoors
and the single brothers sleep each night in sparkling fields
and all wear caps of violet and fuchsia and emerald.

As I light my meager lantern each night and skulk down
the stairs to throw my pick into the lifeless chalk beneath
the Single Brothers basement, I dream not of the expanded
quarters in which we'll dwell, nor of the greater hall

where we'll gather, but of digging so deep into sorrel
earth that I'll tap the floor of those other brothers'
cellar, and when they come for a moment of respite
from all their world's brilliance, they'll hear my knock

and pull me from the clay, and my feet will stand
on ground that sits above its sun, and I'll descend
the stairs to the hall where cold is housed, throw open
the doors to their prismatic Salem, and be home.

And in expectation of that moment, as if to signal
that I have longed to walk among those brothers, I wear
each night a cap of spirited red, the color of the blood
I know will return to my cheeks when I arrive.

My Lydia

—JULIA RIDLEY SMITH—

Late one Saturday night in 1968, young Vera Harrington was driving home from Raleigh to High Point. It had rained heavily most of the way, but by the time she neared Jamestown, the downpour had subsided. A thick fog obscured the familiar landscape, and the lonely road felt strange. Her mother had wanted her home by nine. But Vera was twenty years old, not a child.

Creeping along, she could see only a few feet of road glistening before her headlights. Just beyond the scrap of road, a gray-white wall pressed in like a pillow, smothering. Despite not being able to see her surroundings, Vera thought she must be nearing the spot where—as her grandma used to tell her—the ghost of a long-dead girl hailed cars on rainy nights. Her grandma was full of stories like that. Her grandma also kept a rabbit's foot in her pocketbook and had a horseshoe nailed up over her front door.

"Goddammit!" Vera cried, stomping hard on the brake. A woman in a white dress *had* suddenly appeared in the road! As soon as the car stopped, the woman ran around to the passenger side and slapped at the glass. Vera reached across and rolled down the window.

"I could've killed you!" she fussed. "What the hell are you doing out here?"

"But—are you? Why, you're a girl!" the woman exclaimed,

looking incredulously from Vera's blue jeans to her long hair as though they didn't go together.

"I don't know what the big deal is," said Vera. "So are you!"

It was true. The woman appeared to be no older than Vera herself. Pretty, with wide, pleading eyes and dark bobbed hair. The two girls studied each other for a moment, each assuring herself the other was real. Then the girl in white said she really needed a ride home.

"I don't live far from here. Can you help me?"

Vera sighed. "I guess so. Get in."

The car was old and there was a trick to opening the passenger door. Only Vera had the touch. She hopped out and ran around to let the girl in. The fog pressed so close she could barely make out the edge of the road. It really was a nasty night. She shouldn't have snapped at the lost girl. Back in the driver's seat, she tried to sound more friendly.

"That's a cool dress. I like the fringe."

"Me too." The girl combed the fringe with her slender fingers. "It shimmies when I dance."

"My name's Vera."

"I'm Lydia."

"You want a cigarette, Lydia?"

Lydia gave the merest ghost of a smile. "I haven't had a cigarette in ages. I'd love one."

Vera lit two cigarettes and handed one over. As Lydia took a drag and exhaled a pleased cloud of smoke, Vera laughed.

What a coincidence! A girl stranded near the very underpass Vera's grandma talked about in her crazy story. She pictured asking her grandma: Do ghosts smoke cigarettes? Or wear ridiculous little high-heeled shoes and carry silly beaded clutch handbags? Vera was pretty sure ghosts didn't have feet. Or wallets. Or lungs.

Vera laughed. "You really did scare the bejesus out of me, Lydia.

Jumping out in the road like that. I mean, I almost peed in my pants."

Not a chuckle. No *Sorry I almost scared the pee out of you.* No *Thank you for the cigarette.* Lydia just puffed and stared moodily out into the vast nothingness. Now who was unfriendly?

Oh well. Let it go. Hadn't Vera's boyfriend said that same evening how she needed to be more live and let live? More peace and love?

She resumed driving slowly through the fog. "So where is it I'm taking you?"

Lydia gave directions. Vera knew the area she was talking about, a street of houses with big yards, the houses set well back from the road.

"So did your car break down or what?"

"My *life* broke down," Lydia said. "I was at a dance with this boy. We were having a real good time. And then it all went to hell."

Vera nodded sympathetically. She knew all about the ways a night out with a boy could go to hell. For instance, when you drive two whole hours to hear your boyfriend's half-baked Doors cover band only to discover after the show that he's got his arm around another girl.

"The funny part is," Lydia said, "he was the first boy my mother actually *wanted* me to go out with. She thought he was a catch."

"But he turned out to be the kind you throw back?"

"The kind you *hurl* back," she seethed, her tone turning so vicious as she spoke that Vera wondered for a moment if Lydia had done something horrible to the disappointing boy, out there in the foggy thicket off the highway. Her dress was spotless, though, and her thin arms looked weak.

"Did you fight? And he left you out there all by yourself?"

Instead of answering, Lydia said, "You know, Vera, not too many girls drive around alone at this hour."

"Oh, my mama's probably called the highway patrol by now. But I have to live! I can't just sit around the house every night."

"Of course not!" Lydia agreed. "My mother's the same way. Worry, worry, worry. She can't just let me be. Why can't she just let me be?"

Again her tone dropped into a quiet seething bitterness that made it hard for Vera to know what to say next. If only she could drive faster down this oppressive road. All she wanted was to get this girl where she needed to be and then get her own tired self home.

They crept along until Lydia finally pointed at a mailbox. "Turn there."

At the end of a rutted, muddy driveway stood a two-story, white wooden house. Maybe it had been nice once. Maybe.

"Thanks for the ride," Lydia said. She fumbled helplessly with the door handle.

"Hold on," Vera said. "I'll help you."

As she stepped out, her foot plunged straight into cold water, ankle-deep. Vera cussed, and then, cussing some more, maneuvered awkwardly out of the car, trying to avoid putting her other foot in the water. Wary of finding more puddles, she edged slowly around the car to the other side, then wrenched open the passenger door.

Lydia's seat was empty.

Had she managed to open the car door after all? Vera called up toward the unappealing house.

"Hey! Hey, Lydia!"

No sign of her. How annoying. Vera had hoped to use the phone, and maybe the bathroom, before she got back on the road. She climbed the porch steps and knocked.

The front door opened immediately. A very stooped, absurdly old woman glared up at her.

"Why, you're a girl!" the woman said, sounding as surprised as Lydia had.

"Yes, I brought your—" Vera hesitated. How could she say "your daughter" to this woman? She was old as dirt, way too old to be Lydia's mother. Even Vera's grandma wasn't *this* old.

"I know, I know. You brought Lydia home."

"Did she get in okay?"

"Honey, whenever she gets here, she never shows her face to me." Then she yelled, "Do you, Lydia?"

So Lydia had gotten in. Good. All Vera wanted now was to use the phone, pee, go home, and take off her horrible squishy sock.

"Ma'am, would it be all right if I maybe use your bathroom? And also call my mother? It's so late. I know she's losing her mind by now."

"Aren't you sweet," the woman said, opening the door wider and beckoning her inside. "Aren't you thoughtful! Imagine that! Calling your folks so they won't worry!"

Again nobody answered the woman's yelling. Probably Lydia had already ditched her shoes and fancy dress and was now cozy in her bed, lucky duck.

The old woman led Vera through a hall black as pitch, past a looming shadow that she realized with relief was only a coat-rack, then past another, even more looming shadow that proved to be a staircase. If there was a bathroom in this creepy old tomb, Vera wasn't eager to visit it. She'd just have to hold it until she got home.

In the back room an oil lamp left over from the last century burned on a round table next to an uncurtained window. The lamp's glass globe was etched with forget-me-nots. The woman sat and gestured to the chair opposite.

"Sit down. I want to show you something."

"I really should call my mother," Vera said, but she had no clue how to disobey such an ancient person. She sat. The worn paisley tablecloth reminded her of a fortune teller's shawl. She hoped the old woman wasn't going to gaze into the globe and tell her future.

"My Lydia was always so hardheaded and wild. Buck wild! Did whatever she liked. I couldn't stop her, and her daddy couldn't stop her either. He was in the war, you see, and when he came back, he wasn't in his right mind. Couldn't work, couldn't lift a finger around the place. I had to take care of everything. I couldn't be watching the girl all the time."

Vera fingered the tablecloth's red swirls and blue dots. "I went to protest the war today."

The old woman waved her bony hand dismissively. "Won't do a lick of good," she scoffed. "There's not a thing we can do to stop these crazy men making wars."

Vera thought about her uncles who went to France to stop Hitler. One had come home with a limp and a cast-lead model of the Eiffel Tower. The other had not come back.

"I used to look at Lydia and think, at least she won't go off and get killed in a war. Little did I know."

The old woman opened a thick album lying between them on the table.

"There she is, my Lydia, and there. And there, and there." She turned the pages. Sepia photographs on thick cards. A baby in a christening gown. A small girl with a hair bow that made her head look like it had sprouted wings. A bigger, sulking girl in a sailor blouse.

A frightfully weird tightness seeped through Vera's chest, up her neck, and into her jaw.

"I always dressed my Lydia like an angel, even after I knew she was a devil," the old woman said. Her bony finger came to rest on a picture of the slim young woman who'd been sitting in Vera's car moments before. Same bobbed dark hair. The fringed white dress. The high heels. The last photo in the album was dated 1923.

"She went to a dance," Vera murmured, remembering how her grandma would say the words so theatrically, relishing the tragedy. "Your only daughter."

"My only daughter," Lydia's mother agreed, finally sounding sad. "She went to a dance."

Vera went on, the tightness gripping her throat: "There was an accident."

She looked into the old woman's eyes to see could it all really be true.

"There was a *terrible* accident," the old woman said. "Near the underpass."

Her eyes were full of pain.

"That's where I picked her up," Vera said.

The woman's eyes narrowed. Sharpened. Lydia's mother slammed the album shut.

"That's always where they pick her up! That tease slinks out of the fog at them, showing her leg like Claudette Colbert... Shameless! Always running around—to dances, to races, out to the swimming hole—going with any boy who has a car and a dollar in his pocket. Everybody talking about how boy crazy she is—"

Outside, a white shape flitted past the uncurtained window. Not a flash of lightning, Vera realized with a jolt, but a person. She jumped up.

"Ma'am, I'd better go—my mother—"

"My mother will be *so worried*, she tells them. Like she ever cared if I was worried! And just what are those men doing picking up young girls in the middle of the night? You don't have to tell me. Why, every time there's a storm, I know there's going to be another one knocking on my door, licking his chops, wanting to know where did my Lydia—"

The white shape materialized at the window again. Lydia

peered in, eyes blazing at Vera, pale hands soundlessly striking the glass.

"There!" Vera pointed.

The mother didn't turn. She only had eyes for Vera now. Her speech became plaintive, urgent, as though whatever happened next hinged on getting Vera to comprehend what her life had been all these years.

"Why, I haven't had a lick of peace since my Lydia was born! She was a trial to me living, and she's a trial to me dead."

"Turn around!" Vera insisted. "She's there! Behind you!"

"I know! But she won't be if I turn around. And she'll never come inside!"

Vera ran to the window and touched the cold glass. Nothing. The girl had vanished once more into the fog.

"Used to just kill her daddy, hearing those men asking, 'Did Lydia get inside all right?' In the end, it really did kill him. And *still* she didn't come inside. Forty-five years it's been now, and the men keep coming, and every time, I can't help myself, I always open the door. I think maybe this time. But she never comes inside!"

Lydia's mother threw back her head and shouted to the rafters, "Fine with me! I don't want you in here anyway! Do you hear me? I wouldn't *let* you in here!"

What were they doing? This half-dead woman and her ghost of a girl?

"But now you're here," said the mother, smiling at Vera in a way that instantly made her dart back toward the door.

"Please!" the mother begged, following her. "It's wonderful to have a *nice* girl to talk to. Don't go back out in that nasty weather. Wait until the morning. You can stay in Lydia's room."

As soon as Lydia's mother said those words, a howl arose outside. For a second—but only for a second—Vera thought it must be the wind. Then the sound grew louder, shaking the walls of the decrepit house, and there could be no mistaking what it was.

Vera groped and stumbled through the abysmal hall. Behind her, the mother pleaded, "Oh, do stay."

Not wind, but voice: a once-human wailing voice, offering no words, only an awful piteous endless outraged warning, wailing lament...

"Honey, please. Stay! *Stay!*"

And just as Vera felt a hand clutch her sleeve, the front door blasted open, and she bolted through it, free.

The Kirk Road Bridge

—ED SOUTHERN—

Maybe this'll keep the nosy bastards away at last, Clyde thought. He'd have thought that the thought would've made him smile, but he sat grim-lipped as usual while the yellow trackhoe arm plucked the timbers of the Kirk Road Bridge like dandelions. On the far side, the town side, of trickly Kirk Branch sat the two concrete pipe culverts the NCDOT crew soon would lay, once that damn bridge was no more.

Clyde sat a while. *Maybe this'll keep 'em away at last*, he thought. *Maybe, at last, Nancy will be able to sleep a night.* The hydraulic arm plucked a big section, the timbers somehow holding together like they had a will, and for a few seconds the bridge entire seemed to be flying, floating in the soggy summer air. Then the bucket dropped out from under it, and the Kirk Road Bridge—the famous Kirk Road Bridge, the haunted Kirk Road Bridge, the goddamned all to hell Kirk Road Bridge—crashed into the dump truck below.

'Bout damn time, Clyde thought. *No, long past time. Good goddamn riddance.*

He backed his Buick in a slicing arc, until the rear wheels crunched gravel and grass, and turned to take the back way into town.

Halloweens were the worst, of course, but they never stopped for any season, not for the last fifty years. Teenagers, mostly—still, always, till Kingdom Come—though lately he'd seen more and more grown-ass adults, middle-aged or older, older even than Clyde. They'd bring their damn kids, or maybe grandkids. They were from here, or from near here, but then they'd gone off to Charlotte or Raleigh or wherever else for jobs. They were back in town showing their families where they'd grown up, showing them the Kirk Road Bridge, famous if you were from here, telling them one or the other of the scary stories gathered to it through the years.

Drive slow across on a moonless night, and when you get home you'll find your car covered with the handprints of ghostly children.

Park your car in the middle of the bridge on a night of the full moon. Cut your engine and whistle "Dixie." Turn the ignition again and listen to your engine sputter and cough and refuse to turn, not till you've gotten out and pushed it off the bridge.

Drive up to the bridge on a night of the new moon and cut your headlights. The ghosts of Kirk Road will appear all about you, rapping and scratching at your windows and doors. Your headlights won't come back on until you're across the bridge.

Worse yet than the returning natives were those who'd begun showing up the last several years, calling themselves "ghost hunters" or such, bringing fancy cameras and big fuzzy microphones for what they said was "YooHoo" or "U-Boat" or something. These, Clyde figured, had seen that silly *Ghostbusters* movie when they were too young to know nonsense when they saw it. They came with gadgets they said could measure the energy in the air.

"Like any tool could measure evil," Clyde had taken to saying to those, after seeing how silent it made them, until he'd said it to one who'd whooped and whoa-ed and laughed a laugh that sounded like a goat throwing up.

Clyde had learned at last to sleep through the midnight visits, the brays and hollers and clinks of the empty bottles he'd collect in the morning. Nancy never had. Her big brown eyes would go wide, and sometimes he could see them glisten in the seeping light from the cars. Some nights, she'd moan so low Clyde could think or pretend it was the sound of something else, a lonesome bird or distant motor. Most nights, though, she'd go to their bedroom window, rattle and slap the glass. Clyde worried that some night she'd go down there and stand before them in her nightgown right there on the bridge. He didn't know what might happen if she did, but he worried on it.

Maybe now, he thought, *with the bridge gone, finally, at last…*

Ray said, "Now there's a man who'd know," near about hollered it, while the bell chained to the door still rang. The two sounds, voice and metal, mingled and obscured each other, made each of them uncertain. Half the heads in the Bojangles turned to Clyde.

Of course they're talking about the damn bridge, Clyde thought. All the usual fellas were there, tucked up in their usual corner, along with a younger but not young man whose face Clyde knew but could not place. *I should've known. And I should've gone to the McDonald's.* He gave the girl behind the counter his order.

"Big doings out your way today," Jerry said.

Clyde grunted as he set down his tray on a table an arm's reach from the fellas' booth.

"They're tearing down a vital piece of county history," Ray said. He winked at Gary as he said it. He made sure all the fellas saw him wink.

"How much work they got done so far?" Gary asked Clyde.

"Near about gone," Clyde said. "They done took the most of it already."

"Huh," Ricky said. "I figured it'd take 'em forever and a day."

"Way the government works," Jerry said.

"Uh-huh."

"Ain't that the truth."

"They ain't finished it yet, now," Ray said. "Man said it's only mostly gone. Might take 'em till Christmas just to get the pilings."

"Got that right."

"You might be taking the long way 'round the rest of your life, Clyde."

"Shoot yeah."

"NCDOT got all them Mexicans working for 'em now."

"Shoot, Mexicans is better'n all them," Gary said, then glanced across the Bojangles and lowered his voice, "affirmative action hires."

The fellas hummed in near harmony.

"So what we were wanting to know," Ray said. "My new preacher here hatn't heard the story of the Kirk Road Bridge."

"No," the younger-but-not-young preacher said, a laugh like a buckler lurking in his voice, "that ain't the problem." To Clyde his "ain't" sort of flapped in the air like the cuffs of his daddy's suit coat on a child playing dress-up. "The problem is that I've heard all kinds of stories about how the Kirk Road Bridge came to be haunted, and I don't know which one is the true story."

Clyde considered him less than a second. "The true story?"

The preacher blinked and drew breath to answer, but Ray spoke first.

"So what all stories have you heard?"

Ricky answered before the preacher could.

"I always heard that it was old Mister Kirk that owned a whole plantation out along the creek and gave the branch and road his name. He was known already for his wickedness, known to whip and otherwise mistreat his slaves and never to darken no church house door. But then one day he comes to find out that one of his daughters…"

"His oldest daughter."

"He had five of 'em."

"…finds out that the oldest of his five daughters has done got herself in the family way…"

"By one of his own slaves," Gary said like a blister popping.

"By one of his slaves," Ricky said. "So old Mister Kirk, he goes plumb crazy. He waits for his wife and all five of his girls to sit down for supper, and then he locks the door, pulls out his long knife, and one by one he slits their throats. Then he goes out to the slave cabin out back, bolts the door shut, and lights it on fire, burning up not just the one that compromised his daughter but all of 'em, burning 'em up alive."

"And what happened to him?" the new preacher asked.

The silence lasted only a second.

"What my mama told me," Jerry said, "was that sometime in the Depression, a different Mister Kirk—a descendant, I guess, of that old Mister Kirk—went crazy one night. He tied his wife to a rocking chair in the parlor, and one by one he brought their children in and had 'em kiss her good night. Then, while she watched, all tied up and helpless, he took his Case knife and slit their throats, one by one. When at last he'd done the baby of the family he kissed her good night, too, just like he'd made the kids do, and slit her throat, and then he shot himself. Only one to live was the oldest girl 'cause she was out on a date that night."

"Naw, he didn't shoot himself right there," Gary said. "He went down to the branch to wash the blood off his hands. When it wouldn't come off, that's when he shot himself."

"And that's why every full moon," Ricky said, "Kirk Branch runs red."

Clyde looked to Ray's new pastor. He was grinning a tight grin, but grinning with what, Clyde couldn't tell. He sort of hoped the preacher was grinning with discomfort, unease at the ease with which the fellas talked of such bloody things.

"That all never happened out our way," Clyde said. "That was over to Brook Cove, and the family was the Lawsons. My great-grandmother went to church with them, knew the one who lived. And that wasn't no girl, but the oldest son that was out on a date."

"But that all actually happened," the pastor said, "just not where he said it did?"

Clyde shrugged. "Pretty much."

Clyde remembered how once, as a boy of maybe twelve, he was listening to his daddy play some old songs on his guitar while his mama sang: "Omie Wise," "Pretty Polly," "Poor Ellen Smith," "Tom Dooley." Of a sudden he'd had the thought how odd it was to have all these beautiful songs about the ugliest of sins, about cold-blooded murder, about the full depths of depravity.

He'd had the thought like a question, *What sort of a people would sing of such as that?*

"None of that is what happened on the Kirk Road Bridge," Ray near about hollered. Half the heads in the Bojangles turned once more. Clyde's head turned to see Ray staring at him, hard, but with a hint of a smile on his lips.

"What happened," Ray said, "and Clyde, you tell 'em if this ain't the truth, is that one night..."

And he told them all—the fellas and the new preacher and anyone in the Bojangles who chose or couldn't help but to listen—the facts and the truth of what had happened by the Kirk Road Bridge.

Clyde didn't quit breathing hard till he was halfway home. The punch had surprised himself as much as it had Ray. He didn't think he'd hurt Ray much. He'd gone for his jaw, not his nose or lips. Ray was an old man now, but so was Clyde.

He didn't mind or wonder much at how people could take a real horror that had happened to real people and turn it into a story. He figured that was just what people did, a big part of how they stayed people. He minded and wondered greatly how people could turn such a horror into nothing *but* a story, an entertainment sung or told, and do it so soon, so easy, so gleeful.

Ray had liked to lick his lips when he got into the telling: How it was old man Milo Andrews, not no Kirk, that did the deed that cursed and hainted the bridge; how the deed he'd done he'd done to no one but himself; how he'd parked his old pickup truck afore the bridge, beside the branch, backed up so he could gaze out on the trickling water as he laid down in the truck bed, lit a stick of dynamite he'd took from a road crew site, and stuck it in his mouth like a cigar.

Once upon a time, Clyde had told that story himself, easy and gleeful as Ray. Back when they were teenagers, he and Ray and some other fellas, teammates on the football and baseball teams, had drove out to the Kirk Road Bridge when the moon was full. He'd tossed his pop-tops and empties into the branch. He'd cut his engine and whistled "Dixie" and waited for the haint, for the curse, for the supernatural something like justice to be done, for the spirits of the air to visit upon him and his kind the vengeance he knew the law of the land never would.

Nothing had happened, except they'd got drunk.

Three nights later he'd met Nancy.

Nancy was Milo's youngest daughter, a child when he'd done what he did but old enough to remember him before, to remember him fiddling and singing, to remember him happy—old enough to remember the horror of what he'd done. The sadness of it had made her eyes moonlike, even when she smiled and laughed, which she did more often than you might expect. He'd fallen in love with those moonlike eyes, brown and deep and rich as ponds, round and distant as the full moon. For her eyes and his love he'd quit singing and playing guitar since it only drug up her memories of her father, of how he'd been, of what he'd done.

She'd just as soon not have lived in her family's house on her family's land, so close to where her father had done what he did. Neither one of them would've, but the house and the land had passed to her, and free land and a house upon it is hard to say no to. They'd managed to build a life together, though, each hard day and month and year at a time, each time they laid with or laid into one another; through the layoffs at the hosiery mill and the cigarette plant, through each loss, each illness, up to and after that last one.

Clyde drove past his driveway to see what was left of the bridge. What was left was nothing. The fellas were full of shit: the DOT crew of Blacks and Mexicans and whoever else had worked hard and well that morning.

Clyde went home and went on about his day, took on the pointless projects, the useless repairs of a man retired before he meant to be.

At last the summer sun was down and Clyde let himself climb the creaky stairs to his bedroom, the room he still shared with Nancy. From the window, with the curtains drawn, he could look down to the branch, but even with the hunter's moon he couldn't see if they'd laid the culverts or if the waters rolled free and uncovered one last night.

He knew the bridge was gone, though. He'd seen that in the daytime. *Please, Lord,* he thought and maybe prayed, *please, Lord, let Nancy get some rest now.*

He pulled the covers to his chin.

He switched off the bedside lamp.

He closed his eyes.

He heard the old rattling.

Bridge or no bridge, the curse carried on.

He heard Nancy's palm slapping against the window glass, and he squeezed tight the eyes he'd already shut. He lay like that he didn't know how long, listening to her slap, listening to her rattle.

At last he opened one of his eyes to look into Nancy's, moon-like, brown and shining and sad, floating outside their bedroom window.

Would You Miss Me?

—TYREE DAYE—

I'm far away from my living, the dead
in me are birds,

the wind finally gave my uncle wings.
I hope this storm miles off will carry me to him,
the heart is not a cardinal, it can't leave on its own
without the body.

If wings grew out of my back
my heart couldn't take their beating, so I feed the birds
parts of me no one called beautiful,
            my father's moon of a nose.

I made a room of my grief.
When you ask to enter
                        it changes itself into a room half its size.

If I didn't return the way snowbirds return with snow,
songbirds return songs to one another across a harvested field,

the way my grandmother returns to my dreams begging me
to let her stay dead.

The light returning to her face in minutes.

from Cardinal, *Copper Canyon Press*, 2020

Uncle Gig's Return

—TYREE DAYE—

Uncle Gig stole a flashlight from Uncle Pac's shed
and cast himself on the side of my mama's porch
my mama said it was gift
            like a rat in your house is a gift

I was told not to see him
but I was diamond-headed

he swelled in me like a river
because I was a drought expecting to happen

to witness it would have made you find your own uncle
on a bus looking for your grave

he was indistinguishable from a lizard
on your daddy's shoulder

from a little bump in the earth, *Copper Canyon Press, 2024*

A House of Vine and Shadow

PART THREE — CHESTNUT

"Is that enough?" the old man said, looking at the woman.

"Oh, good heavens, no."

"I done told you before, woman, ain't but two stories in the whole wide world."

"Foot, if that were so, might as well say all music is just the same seven notes."

Nate heard music then. He heard music coming from his right side, from the corner of the parlor to his right and behind him, and he turned his head to look, but he found the turning hard, and slow, his neck stiff in an unfamiliar way. This wasn't the stiff neck he got from staring at a screen too long for work or gaming or from sleeping funny or not stretching at the gym. This was a stiff neck like his spine was fusing, or decaying, or transforming toward some alien purpose.

When he finally got his gaze around to the corner, he saw a record player spinning a vinyl album. He'd half expected that, but what he'd imagined was some antique Victrola with a hand-turned crank to the side and an ornate trumpet rising above. The record player he saw was a hi-fi stereo, much like the one his more well-off set of grandparents had owned but rarely played.

He set his head off on the journey away from the corner, back toward the old couple. He set his mouth to try to speak: "I'm … Nate Batts … Goldleaf … more than fair …"

He felt now, though, not as if he were swimming against a strong current but as if a whole river was beating down on his head, as if he was looking up into a torrent, a waterfall, and he'd somehow have to climb it, ascend the water itself, if he ever were to breathe again.

At last his head and eyes returned to the old couple on the sofa. The woman smiled and breathed deep.

"I do so love the smell of chestnut. I've missed it so."

"Dear," the old man said, "that's the mountain laurel blooming that you smell."

"No, it's the chestnut, dear."

"Chestnut's dead, my dear, all dead, long dead."

"Not so, no more dead than them that..."

When she paused, she turned her glance again to Nate, and though she smiled, Nate felt a flutter, a quiver, a shudder run all his length down, from the back of his nose to the heels he knew were glued to the floor somehow.

He said, "I'd like... I need... go... now," though as each word staggered from his lips he knew he never would.

The old woman turned to face him full. She widened her smile, and Nate moaned.

She said, "You see, many who pass ain't dead, or ain't dead and gone at least. They ain't gone nowhere and won't never..."

Chimney Rocket

—JEREMY B. JONES—

Patsey Reaves, a widow woman, who lives near the Appalachian Mountain, declared, that on the 31st of July last, about 6 o'clock p.m., her daughter Elizabeth, about eight years old, was in the Cottonfield, about 10 poles from the dwelling house, which stands by computation, 6 furlongs from the Chimney Mountain, and Elizabeth told her brother Morgan, aged 11 years, that there was a man on the mountain. Morgan was incredulous at first; but the little girl affirmed it, and said she saw him rolling rocks or picking up sticks, adding that she saw a heap of people. Morgan went to the place where she was and, calling out, said he saw a thousand or ten thousand flying things in the air.... Mrs. Reaves says she went about 3 poles towards them, and, without any sensible alarm or fright, she turned towards Chimney Mountain and discovered a very numerous crowd of beings resembling the human species.

—*Raleigh Register,* September 15, 1806

The old man and his wife had been seated in their yard, in the deepest portion of the Chimney Rock Pass. Their attention was arrested by the astounding spectacle ... two opposing armies of horsemen, high up in the air, all mounted on winged horses and preparing for combat.

—Silas McDowell papers, 1811

I'd not eaten enough the day he went. That's the first thing. I'd gotten sour with Mama for reasons that you wouldn't understand and so I punished her the best way I knew how: by not eating all the mashed potatoes I'd rightfully heaped of a Monday night. *Fine*, I'm sure I said before pounding off to my room, my body free-falling onto the bed. And there it stayed until the morning.

An empty stomach brings with it dreams of bizarre shapes and sizes. At least that's how it's always been for me. Hunger dreams. Unsatiated nocturnes. It's a sleep state off-kilter because it lacks the proper nutrition to fully substantiate the world it's building. It's a wonky, half constructed place. That night there had been gauzy pink skies and a tiny version of me who refused to speak, but only stared. And McDonald's french fries. Those I remember because they seemed the shiniest things around, like they'd been wet with a fire hose before man-sized saltshakers rained down. *Manna from McHeaven*, dream-me said to mini-me, but the little creep didn't even smile.

Anyhow, what I'm saying is that I came back to this world, the one without shrunken versions of me, in a right strange way the next morning. *Queer* is how my grandpap would've called it, though he'd've said it in a way that sucked in the cheeks and rounded out the mouth and was very nearly the word *choir*. The point is, I couldn't be sure of anything when my eyes opened and the early sun spilt right into the room. Even Mama's silhouette couldn't be trusted at that first light, her body craning over me and saying, "Holt" over and over. She might've been a renegade french fry turning the tables on the food chain.

I did come to, eventually. I covered my head and told her, "Quit it with all that."

"Get up," she said in a way that was not wholly unlike how she might have said it on any Tuesday morning, though I detected a note off-key in her pleas. It might've been panic if Mama had the capacity for such.

"Daniel's gone," she said, returning to the usual matter-of-factness that governed her head to toe.

"Who's Daniel," I might've said because I was wrong about being wholly out of the pink-french-fry land. Even as I sat up and registered Mama's tight perm over me, I was a foot in two worlds. I know now, of course, Daniel is my baby brother. A clumsy crybaby of six. Good, glorious riddance.

"Get your britches on and find your brother."

What I like best is when the sky is like dry ice. After a wet night, the clouds stick to the mountains and stretch like cotton when the morning sun emerges to try to burn them out. The clouds thin and pull apart and eat up trees. What it is is the perfect way for Joe Elliott to step onto stage, scream-sing *In the beginning God made the land.* Lights and leather and a one-armed drummer and those mountain morning skies under their feet as if they're floating above my house like the angels they are and forever will be. Amen.

That's how the clouds were that morning, and come to think of it, Chimney Rock would be the perfect stage. It juts above and beyond this gorge I had no choice but to be born into, a flat top for the band to absolutely rain down *a satellite of love* on everything cutting between these bluffs: my little house hanging up the mountainside, this town that ain't a town but instead a scattering of houses and a strip of wooden tourist traps, and, somewhere out there, my vanished brother. And my vanished daddy. And my vanished grandpap.

Daniel wasn't really vanished. He just wanted attention. Or else he forgot how to walk and just rolled down the mountain into the river and got carried downstream until his roly-poly body was deposited into Lake Lure, where it floated or sank or maybe just became water and did what it was supposed to do. Or maybe he'd become one of the ghost townspeople down there on the lake bottom.

Grandpap wasn't vanished either. Just dead. He's the one who told me about all the ghosts in the lake, about the town that had been there before the river was dammed and the souls that carried on living beneath the water. He told me too about the treasure that had been buried somewhere up the mountain, stashed there by redcoats or conquistadors or some other white settlers just before they were cut down in battle. I should say, he told me about all this before he died. I haven't talked to him since he croaked, but I'll admit I am open-minded about convening with the passed-on. I have some questions.

Which is to say I wasn't looking for Daniel. Not really. I was walking. I was strolling amid a blessed metal morning of dry ice clouds. Besides, where would he go if he'd gone? He couldn't read. He didn't have money. He couldn't even tie his stupid Velcro shoes.

But I could hear Mama calling his name back towards the road, so I reckoned I owed it to her to call out just the same. That's how come Jason stepped out of the woods out near the rock we called Gremlin. He'd heard me half-heartedly calling my brother's name and appeared like Beetlejuice.

"You playing Manhunter?" he said first thing.

Manhunter was the jacked-up version of hide-and-seek we played at night. We'd chase each other through swarms of rhododendron and the hundreds of acres stretching up the mountain. Jason always wanted to use flashlights, but that was soft. I liked it best when our eyes had to adjust, when we had to be animals in the pitch black.

"Nah, Mom is making me look for Daniel," I said. He fell in beside me as we picked our way across the stream we called Slow Roll.

"You get to skip school?"

Jason was in sixth grade like me and was about the closest thing I had to a best friend, but he wasn't what Mrs. Edney would call the creamsicle of the crop. He'd stepped off the bus with me last week on the last day of school, singing *teachers leave them kids alone* but all twangy like it was an Alan Jackson song.

"Radical," he said in his best Ninja Turtle voice when I reminded him school was out for summer.

After a while, I turned us back towards home. I couldn't hear Mama anymore, and I was hungry. Daniel was probably eating Fruit Loops on the couch by now anyhow.

"Man, Daniel always runs away," Jason said as we picked up the trail we'd cut over the years, the one that runs up towards the backside of Chimney Rock, the side the tourists don't know how to find.

"Nah, not really. He's never run away."

"Oh... weird."

Swear to God, I'd not thought of it until then. Or maybe some tucked-away part of my brain had, but I'd just kept tucking it away. Like I say, hunger. Truth was, Daniel whined all the time and couldn't eat anything without dropping half of it on the floor, but he was always underfoot. Always in the way, either stuck to Mama or me. Vanishing without a word wasn't like him at all.

That was the moment when something slippery happened in my chest and I wondered if I ought to have been hollering for real and looking down the mountainside instead of talking about if Sergeant Slaughter could kill a triceratops. I told Jason I'd call him later and ran home at Manhunter speed.

It was mostly volunteer firefighters at first, but before long sheriff's deputies and EMTs and the Barnwell brothers that hunt this land spread out around us. A few of them had dogs. I *wasn't to leave this house*, which felt kindly shortsighted on Mama's part. What could happen to me out there? Some fireman's gonna kidnap me away? Them woods was probably the safest place in the whole county that afternoon.

I was a good enough kid. Mrs. Edney let me take the erasers outside on Fridays. I sat still when we were made to sit still. I gave it my all in crab soccer. Sure, I had my run-ins with writing sentences and sitting in the hall, but for the most part, I followed the rules. "You're hardly anything like your daddy," Mrs. Williamson, the music teacher, told me once, and I didn't know just what it meant—the man was more of a memory than any kind of flesh and blood—but I knew enough to know it was meant as a compliment.

But when night come on and there was still no Daniel and Mama had been crying on the couch and all them men had their flashlights out, I waited until some volunteer came in to pee and I slipped out the back door behind him before it slapped closed. I couldn't sit still any longer.

It goes without saying that there was no search party when Lemuel Johnson Sr., absconded of a summer day. Those men with flashlights that I avoided as I snuck out hadn't combed the mountainside three years ago when he'd gone, leaving me back here with the damn name Lemuel Jr. Let the record show that anybody who knows anything knows never to call me that. I've been Holt since I could talk, but still. That thing will be on my driver's license one day. I'll have to tell it to some girl when she wants to know the real me.

They wouldn't have found him back then, search party or no. Nobody believed he'd gone missing, only that he'd took off. I'm not ashamed to say that I looked for him all up through here, stepping into caves and dark corners whispering, "Daddy," but I let all that go when I turned eleven. Truth be told, I hardly think about the man or the memory anymore.

For a pro like me, it was easy to steer clear of the searchers. They were noisy and bright as lighthouses, and I'd slid through that dark more times than I could count. It was weird, though: disappearing so that I could find my disappeared brother. I was both the hider and the seeker. And I had no earthly where to look. I decided I'd go to the darkest places, to the spots where I could not be seen and where no one else was hunting. If I had it to do over again, maybe I'd decide different, but what's done is done. I set out blind, dumb to what waited up that mountainside.

What I like about that nighttime dark is that the world is cut right down to shapes. It's simpler. There aren't trees or rocks; there are lines. Yes, there are pine needles whacking me in the face and rocks rough enough to turn my palms white, but I know those by touch, not sight. What I'm saying is there's not a lot of thinking, only moving and reacting. The strange summertime music of frogs and cicadas surrounds you so that it's hard to know what's coming from where; you're just out there in it, and you have to accept that you don't ever fully know just what *it* is. A scream or a fox. A screech owl or banshee. A far-off dog or a coyote calling the pack to you. It ought to be terrifying, but it's always been a kind of freedom for me. A kind of letting go.

Once I got into the woods, my head downshifted to that nighttime mode of evasion, so I wasn't really thinking about what I might find. I wasn't thinking much about what it might mean that Daniel could be somewhere out here, maybe up there on one of the bluffs. He couldn't get up there on his own. He could barely use the bathroom on his own. But I wasn't thinking that if he was out there, he wouldn't be alone, that somebody would've brought him. I didn't think; I just climbed, bushwhacking low and slow.

The thing about Daddy was that he wasn't anybody's villain. I said we all knew he left because he was running away, but it's not like he was some kind of evil madman. No one wanted him to leave, not exactly. He never hit me or Mama, never rode through town shooting a gun or nothing. He was just kindly translucent, never fully here, never solid enough to rely on. In a way, he always reminded me of Face from *A-Team*. He wasn't quite that handsome, but he had something that made people look twice. And he used it. If you were to ask me what he'd done for work, I'd say he talked. That's how it felt then—he talked to people, and they gave him things. Saying it now, I guess it's wrong to say *nobody* wanted him to leave. There was some. People he'd cheated or wronged, but even they never seemed all that mad.

"Your daddy ain't always right," Grandpap used to tell me like it was some life lesson I hadn't already learned a hundred times, but Grandpap had never been taken in by the spell of Lemuel Johnson. He'd allowed it to be cast nonetheless. He'd watched Lemuel marry his daughter and move onto his land, but he'd always spied Daddy with a pinched face, always half squinting like he was looking at something too shiny to fully see.

Mama never said it, but I know she expected Daddy would show up when Grandpap died. I could tell by how she sometimes peered out the window or sat up too quick when the house popped in its nightly settling routine. Dad'd been gone nearly a year by then, but grapevines being what they are, he probably heard tell of James Maxwell's dying. And I didn't know it then, but I later understood that Grandpap's death meant stretches of this gorge now belonged to Mama. Grandpap's now-empty house too. If nothing else, Mama must've figured Daddy would come strolling back in to lap up some of the inherited land. But the door never swung open. His crooked smile never took a seat at the table.

Like I say, that was fine by me. We had no need for his hang-dog ways. The TV worked. We could afford Cap'n Crunch. There weren't nothing he could bring to the Hickory Nut Gorge that we needed.

At first, I couldn't rightly tell if it was one voice or two. I reckoned some searchers had found the path me and Jason cut up the mountain, so I hid behind a sprawl of mountain laurel to watch them pass. But the voice or voices carried on, never quite moving. Eventually, I stepped out from my hiding spot and stood still on the trail, listening. Chimney Rock still towered above me, but by then I'd made my way high enough that it seemed within reach: I could step onto this ridgeline portion of our trail and wind my way easily into the bluffs, the blackness of the gorge like an open mouth down below. The murmurs, though, were coming from somewhere beyond the trail, just downhill, so I cut back into the woods with as light a step as I could manage.

I couldn't get closer. I know it sounds crazy, but no matter how deep I worked into the forest, the voices stayed out of reach. They'd come and go, and I followed their whispers like a hound, but the sounds never drew closer, no matter how far I walked. Was I imagining them? I couldn't blame this here on hunger. Ladies from up at the church in Bat Cave had brought us some casseroles, and I'd eat my fill before it turned dark. But I started to feel like maybe I was dreaming this whole thing and was only now catching on, only now noticing that the world around me was unreal and of my own making.

That didn't stop the whispering. Whether I was imagining it or not, I felt sure it was more than one person. I couldn't make out words, but there was some kind of conversation, all hushed and constant, and all I could think was that whoever had taken Daniel was out there, talking some nonsense to my little lost brother.

"Help," I yelled then because I decided me getting in trouble was outweighed by finding Daniel. "I think he's up here!"

The voices stopped, so I did too. I lay down right there on the wet ground and waited for the lights of deputies. The silence then was about the most terrifying thing I've ever heard. I'd scared everything within earshot so that even the cicadas seemed to stop their alien hum. I waited for whoever had Daniel to come tromping towards me, intending to grab me by the scruff and haul me off to whatever cave he'd used to cage up my brother. I waited for a flashlight or a call back from some volunteer who'd heard me. I waited for something to make sense of any of it.

But all that came were the usual nighttime noises. I imagined the forest as one singular organism, like a deer frozen in place at a strange sound only to finally relax and return to business as usual. The cicadas and frogs covered me up again, and I must've been like that, belly on moss and twigs, for ten minutes before I realized nothing was coming. All I'd done was spook the voices, probably alerted Daniel's kidnapping madman that I was there.

I'd started to push myself up to figure what to do next when I heard the undeniable crinkle of a footstep somewhere behind me. Now it was my turn to freeze. I stayed half stooped like that for ten Mississippis, but when no more sounds came, I figured some possum or coon had just been scuttling back to a tree. I stood, intending to make my way back to the house for help, and there in front of me was the man himself: Face. Lemuel Sr. My good-for-nothing daddy.

"What do you say, son?"

I want to say here and now that this isn't one of those *And-then-I-woke up* stories. It would make more sense if it was. Jason's mama let us watch all kinds of stuff we shouldn't when I stayed over at his house, and this would all be more believable as a nightmare sponsored by *Swamp Thing*. But I want to make clear before we go on that I was as awake as a twelve-year-old boy who's just seen his long-lost father in the middle of the woods could be. Believe me, I took some convincing myself.

"This ain't real," I said to Daddy. He was wearing those jeans and pointy-toed boots he put on when he went into town, not the sort of thing I'd wear for a walk in the woods. His face looked the same but worn. He didn't have a beard exactly, but there was more fuzz there than I'd ever seen, and his eyes was wrapped up in that kind of saggy, tired skin Mama gets after long shifts. There was a tear in the sleeve of that stupid cowboy-looking shirt, the pearl buttons only snapped halfway up.

"Holt, listen here. We got to get moving."

"This ain't real."

His fingers on my arm felt real enough, so I allowed myself to be pulled along as he made his way back to the path. If I hadn't been stunned stupid, I'd have noticed that the whispers had started up again, but all I was noticing was the back of my vanished daddy's head as he looked for the clearest way back through the trees.

Once we were on the path, he slowed and let go of me. With my animal eyes and the moonlight, I saw him smiling that damn crooked smile that I hated so much because even standing here, dumbfounded and—yeah, I'll admit—angry, I still felt warm when he aimed it at me.

"Holt. I can't believe—son, I been missing you something awful."

"This ain't real," the broken record that was my mouth shot back.

"They denied Jesus three times too," he winked, and then he patted me on my numb shoulder. "What the hell is your mama feeding you to grow you this tall. Are you sitting on some grown man's shoulders under them clothes?"

Of the hundreds of questions spinning on the Rolodex of my mind, I pulled the one that felt most pressing: "Have you seen Daniel?"

He kept up his smile, but I noticed it dip slightly because I was practiced in the ways of reading Lemuel Johnson.

"What's it been? A month, two months?" he asked, hand running through his hair.

But I was locked in now, pushing the messy rucksack of emotions balling up in me into the corner and focusing on the here and now. "Daddy, Daniel's out here somewhere. Listen."

I turned back towards the sounds, and he put that hand on me again, holding me at bay.

"Now wait. Let me get a good look at you."

I pulled against his hand and moved back towards the sounds. He let loose, but he didn't follow. The voices were undeniable now, and I swear one of them said *Daniel.*

"One of us has got to run get everybody," I told Daddy, turning back to him. "Somebody's got Daniel out there, so one of us has to stay and one of us has to run back." I could somehow feel the thump of my heart in my head.

He looked back at me, a little sad. "Reckon you are the man of the house now, Junior."

That's when the first one of them appeared. You're going to tell me it was some kind of lightning or a cloud given shape by my fear or exhaustion or whatever, but what it was was a man—or something like a man—sitting on horseback. They were both brighter than white and floating up there above the rocks. Even in my paralyzed state Johnny Cash was singing about ghost riders in the sky somewhere in the mushiest parts of my brain. *Yipee-yi-o.*

It was huge—the horse and the man—and the ghost rider galloped above us, circling Chimney Rock like in orbit, like some giant projection playing out in the sky.

I pulled my eyes away long enough to look at Lemuel. His eyes was fixed up there too, but while my fear was pure shock I registered that his was something different. He wasn't wide-eyed, but his body had taken on something I could only describe as a cower.

"You can't be here," he said in a near whisper without taking his eyes off the sky, and I wasn't sure if he was talking to me or the lightning man.

Of course, my body wanted only to run down the trail until my front door creaked open. But my brain knew that Daniel could be within reach, and if I left this spot, he might be moved. Or worse.

I stood there, deciding between fight or flight, when Daddy turned to me and said it again, this time louder: "You can't be up here, Holt. You gotta run."

But running was about all my daddy knew, and I was nothing like my daddy. I took one sidelong look at the sky and slipped back into the woods. "Daniel," I yelled. I didn't care who heard me now—all I wanted was to find those voices and get my brother home.

I moved as fast as I could, not minding the branches cutting my arms. I tuned out everything but those whispers; I imagined I was some kind of heat-seeking missile let loose.

"Daniel," I hollered again, on target. But all I found was the edge of the mountain. I ran until the land run out and the voices were coming from beyond the ridgeline, out in the openness, where the darkness was only sky and the long fall back to earth. I listened. I ignored the gusts of wind that had started rattling the trees.

It didn't make any sense that anybody could be out there in the nothingness, so I decided they were above me. I climbed, grabbing roots and rocks to scramble upwards, even as the trees bent with the whooshes of air and the ground itself seemed to shift and the sky took on an eerie glow from whatever or whoever was sliding through the empty sky on some conjured steed. I ignored everything and climbed until I felt the hand on my leg.

Some time went missing. That's all I can tell you. One minute I was scrambling up the rock and the next I was on my back, looking up through the kaleidoscope that was the canopy of trees; beyond it, the ghost rider circled, but he was no longer alone. There was heaps of them—some on horses and some walking. I couldn't tell if they was fighting or working together. The sky looked like fireworks, only the explosions were bodies, and the bodies were massive and solid like lit-up glaciers. I lay there watching it like a television until one of them left the hoard and dropped. My body knew before my brain that he was coming for me, his legs slicing through the air so that he seemed like a downed plane, smoke and contrails and all, and my body said to run but my brain marveled, and if it don't beat all, it somehow found the time to think about Def Leppard again—*I can take you through the center of the dark*—before I managed to roll downhill, swallowed up by a tangle of rhododendron.

The ghost rocket man never made impact, not really, but I felt the wind of him—a cold rush of air through the trees that had me shivering despite the summer night. I wish I could say I was thinking of Daniel then, but all I was thinking of was how to get off that mountain alive. I could hide from EMTs and Jason, but I didn't reckon there was any hiding from ghost soldiers mounting an attack from above. The only way out was with speed, and so I readied myself to find the path and fly home.

But there was Daddy again. Breathing hard behind me. Mumbling to himself something about gold and musket fire and retribution, and I knew he'd lost the plot entirely. "It was always going to come to this," he whispered to himself.

"Daddy, we gotta run," it was my turn to say. I stood and he turned his head towards me but didn't look at me square. His eyes was seeing something, but it wasn't me.

"It's happening again," he said.

"What's happening?" I asked, trying to pull any sense out of him, trying to get him moving.

"I dug it up," he said, looking at me for a second, and then some flash of something across his face: "They want us all." Like a geyser, he stood then and screamed like an insane person: "I'm here for the taking!" He spread his arms like he was awaiting a downpour: "I'm here!"

That was all I needed to know. I was most assuredly not there for the taking. I was there to blur through the woods until men with guns was between me and the ghost army.

"I'm here!" he hollered again, and I bolted for the trail.

I knew better. I'd learned about Sodom and Gomorrah and all, and yet I still looked back up that mountain before I tore down the trail. The floating people had clearly heard my daddy, and the ringleader we'd first seen aimed his ghost horse downward and seemed to call out but no sound came from him. Still, I could feel the air change; it grew cool and charged. Some of the others turned too, stopping their circling and pointing their bodies-not-bodies in the direction of Lemuel Johnson Sr., who was out there in the dark hollering for them to come and get him.

I couldn't save him. I couldn't tell if he wanted to be saved. Hell, I couldn't tell if he was even real. Was I to think he'd just been living up here on this mountain for three years without anybody knowing? Just foraging in his zip-up boots and cowboy shirt?

All I knew was that I needed to run before they swooped in and brought whatever was coming.

But then I saw him. Up there on the edge of the rock, illuminated by the ghost squadron readying to divebomb our daddy: Daniel. He just sat there, legs crossed on the edge of a bluff. He didn't seem scared. He didn't seem anything, really. Just entranced like he was watching TV on Saturday morning.

That's how it was that I came to be running up the trail while the ghost riders were descending like some terrible storm. The trees started bending and the ground started rumbling and the air started chilling, but I hugged the ridge and pushed my body upward. I didn't want to call his name for fear I'd startle him and he'd fall. And, naturally, I was afraid the whole army would turn their sights on me if I started yelling my head off while they mustered, so I ran as best I could in the now-frigid air and the gale-force winds. I ran until I felt the rock Daniel perched on, and then I climbed, my shoes searching for purchase as the wind tried to whip me back down.

I could see his back then, and I wanted to holler. I didn't know what the ghost riders would do to Daddy, but I reckoned they'd be coming back whenever they were done. So I called to Daniel. But it wasn't no use. The wind and the snapping branches and some new bizarre whistling covered up all my attempts to yell. Instead I crept to him and put my hand on his back. He stood, turned, and looked at me, and all I can tell you is that he seemed empty. He saw me, and he followed me, but there was no light in those eyes, no bratty six-year-old moving those legs. He came like a zombie, like a sleepwalker. But I didn't care. He was moving and so was I. We were getting off this mountain.

We'd maybe made it around two bends before I saw the first white figure rising back up towards the rocks. It was another one on horseback, this one wearing a cap like they must've done way back when they came in here playing piccolos and wearing high-water pants. I stopped Daniel, and we waited there silent, thinking to let the man rise back up above us. But in a flash, his cloudy eyes turned, and before we could even think to move, he was on us, the horse galloping through the night air and the soldier face-to-face with us. Like the ringleader had done, this one opened his mouth to speak, but nothing came out. My skin rippled, either from cold or fear or some ghost allergy, but all there was was wind.

"I'm going now," Daniel said to the face, and before I knew I was doing it, I stepped in front of my brother, hoping to keep him from whatever comes from mouthing off to a ghost soldier. That was when I lifted off. Not Superman, cape-flapping-behind-me flying but my body levitating right there on the trail. I tried to move my legs, but I felt frozen, literally and figuratively, and then without any of my doing, I floated a few feet down the trail, leaving Daniel dead in front of the horseman and me stuck in midair. The giant icy face opened his mouth again, and again nothing came out, but Daniel leaned his head to the side like he was listening.

"Buried it will stay," he said, his voice only sort of his.

The ghost rider pulled back on his steed, the horse rising up like he was fixing to stomp down on Daniel. I summoned up any latent powers I might have had, but I couldn't move or call out against whatever had me freezing and floating down the trail.

Daniel didn't run or cry out. He just looked up at the giant haint and spoke: "Take him. He's ready."

They say your life flashes before your eyes, but all I got was a slideshow of all the wrongs I'd committed against Daniel. Holding his bedsheets tight so he couldn't escape the bed; telling him Judy Lyda, the woman who always dressed in cow print, was his real mama; letting him play Manhunter with me and Jason but never trying to find him. I wanted to ask Daniel to forgive me for all of it. To get down on my knees. *Don't send me with them! I'm not ready!* I wanted to scream, but I couldn't do anything but watch as the ghost horse settled back on the air-ground and the soldier opened his mouth again. I reckoned if it was my time, this would be an epic way to go. *Tubular*, Jason would say when the news reached him.

But then the ghost rode off, back towards the others, and they all started rising like comets in reverse. They blurred into the sky, back towards Chimney Rock, and one by one they vanished just above that sore thumb of a rock. It took me a beat to realize I was standing again because my body felt sucked dry. I wanted to collapse right then and there, but I watched the army fly upward and blink out one shiny man at a time.

I nearly missed Daddy because they'd surrounded him, two ghost riders carrying him up and others zooming along beside. He wasn't fighting. Maybe he wasn't even alive. He just lay there, like on an invisible bed, and rose and rose and rose.

"Daddy," I tried to yell, but I was hoarse and only Daniel heard.

Daniel turned to me, his eyes still vacant and his voice still all wrong: "It wasn't his. He's going now."

I had a hundred questions, but everything was suddenly too much. I felt my body folding, and I saw the ghosts and Lemuel Sr. disappear just before the whole world followed suit.

When I came to, I was home. This is why you needed to know about the whole *And-then-I-woke up* gambit before. It was indeed morning, and Mama was indeed sitting by my bed, and I wished it had all been a dream, but she told me the story. Some searchers had found me and Daniel up the trail. We were both passed out, and so they carried us home, delivering us to Mama who had cried more in the past day than I'd seen in my whole twelve years. We seemed fine but exhausted, so they put us both to bed and sent everyone home.

"What about Daddy?" I asked as Mama filled me in.

Her baffled face told me all I needed to know about that. I explained to her about his appearing, about the ghost uprising and his ascension. She put on her usual stoic face, but I could see the tears ringing her eyes.

"Get you some sleep, Holt," she eventually said. "It's been an ordeal and you'll be yourself again after some sleep."

It was afternoon when I woke again, and nobody was at my bedside. I went into the kitchen and saw Mama and Daniel eating bologna sandwiches and tater chips. I could tell by the crumbs all over Daniel that he was back.

"Hey," he said, his voice his own again.

I wanted to ask him questions, but I also wanted to just sit down and eat a sandwich. I pulled out my chair, but before I could take it, I heard Jason hollering from outside. I went out to see him.

"Ho-ly," was all he said.

"I know," I said.

We didn't say anything for a while, just kicking rocks and looking into the woods. I didn't want to tell him everything only to see that same confused, sad look on his face that had been on Mama's. But then he looked up towards Chimney Rock and said it: "A whole damn ghost army. Man alive."

I turned to him quickly, expecting him to be making a joke, but he was only staring up at the mountains.

"I know," was all I said again.

When I sat down at the table, Mama hopped up to go get the bread and mayonnaise and all. I wasn't even sure how to capture what my body felt—numbness and relief and fear. I definitely felt hunger, so I decided to focus on only that. I waited patiently for my sandwich and watched Daniel crunch his chips.

I wanted to tell him sorry and thanks. I wanted to ask about all the things—his vanishing, his speaking to ghosts, his sentencing of our father—but I could only think of his trancelike state and wonder if he remembered any of it. Maybe it was a grace if he didn't. Maybe best to never say a word about any of it. Everything was the same now as it had been last week, so what good would it do?

Before Mama had returned, he turned to look at me too. He smiled, and I couldn't help but see a little something of Lemuel Sr. in it. I hadn't noticed it before, how it hung asymmetrical but had a light about it. Maybe that wasn't all bad. We'd be our father's children, whether we liked it or not.

"I'm glad you're back," I said to him in the sappiest brother moment of my life.

He crunched another chip, and then his eyes took on a kind of icy glow before he leaned closer and whispered, "Reckon you are the man of the house now, Junior."

The Lost Guide

—MARK POWELL—

The headwaters of the Chattooga River begin in the steep shadow of Whiteside Mountain east of Highlands, North Carolina, and for three nights, tucked into my sleeping bag at the foot of what the Cherokee people had once called the "Great Blue Wall," I could hear the river running through the porous walls of my dreams. It was the sound of water and the faint echo of voices, a ghostly unsettling sound, and I heard it every time I shut my eyes. I shouldn't have been surprised. My brothers and I had been making an annual pilgrimage down the river for the last twelve years—three days and two nights of paddling and camping—and this would be our thirteenth trip. It was *our* river, we liked to think. We'd all three grown up just south of where I lay tucked into my fleecy bag, which is to say I knew this world intimately—the white pines and red-tailed hawks, the way the wet earth is revealed beneath a lace of teasing fog. If I had a home—spiritual, physical—this was it.

But less so now, I thought, lying there. In the last year I'd come to feel estranged from both this place and myself, and the night before our trip I felt such acutely. Don't ask why. The reasons aren't important for this story, except to say that on the eve of our thirteenth river trip I felt adrift and was looking, maybe, for some sort of anchor, some sort of sign.

I was looking, I realize in hindsight, for a ghost.

I met my brothers and the rest of the group the next day at Sandy Ford, and seven of us put out in a raft and four kayaks. I was in the back of the raft, a new self-bailing boat made from a material called Hypalon and far superior to the old heavy rubber school bus we'd paddled in years past. The water was low, but we glided over the rocks and through the parched rapids. A bright meandering day of cold water and colder beer. That night we camped at Thrift's Ferry, and though the mood was celebratory—there was much laughing and passing around of a bottle of Elijah Craig—I felt the same despondency that had hung over me for the last year. Still, I smiled. I laughed. I took the bottle as it passed me and drank dutifully.

I knew I needed something to shake me awake.

But knew equally well I wasn't likely to find it.

That night it began to rain. It started as a light thumping on the fly of my tent, and by the time I was fully conscious it had settled into a steady drumbeat. It was a blessing. The river, as I've mentioned, was particularly low, and we knew the rain would buoy us: less getting stuck and more having fun. Before drifting back off to sleep I hoped it would rain all night and stop come daylight.

It didn't. Come morning it was still raining, and we dragged ourselves out to make coffee under a tarp hung quickly between the trees. We were soaked and cold but also happy: The river already appeared thicker, more powerful, churning downstream with a force that had been absent just hours before. Getting soaked was a small price to pay for such.

"Let it come," I remember someone saying, "let it come."

The way he repeated it, it sounded almost like an invocation, almost like a prayer. It occurred to me only later that he hadn't specified what it was he was conjuring.

We waited all morning for the rain to lift. By eleven it was clear it wouldn't, at least not anytime soon, and we broke camp and pushed off into the current. It didn't take long for things to go wrong.

First, the river had risen far more than we'd anticipated. The current was less a pulling thread than a torrent, and the kayaks that held the far more skilled and experienced boaters kept floating ahead only to have to wait for us. Second, the lines of the rapids had changed. Or maybe not changed exactly so much as become more critical. Rapids we would have slithered through at lower levels now growled with that deep timeless power that is moving water. Still, we kept the raft pointed downstream and held on, soaked and happy, exhilarated and maybe just a little afraid.

That fear solidified as we neared the Bull. Bull Sluice is a legendary Class V rapid, famed as much for Decapitation Rock—a blade of granite that rises through its center like a giant fin—as for the crowds of folks who hike down to watch boats spill, in the same spirit as people who watch NASCAR for the wrecks. But that day it was empty, eerily empty.

We pulled onto the rocky beach and hiked down to stand on the overhang. Beneath us, the Bull churned water with a power I can only equate to that of the ocean. It was like a tsunami. It was like a fissure had broken in the earth and all its water was spilling out. You had to yell to be heard over it, though the three of us in standing there had nothing to say. The kayakers were downriver, no doubt pushed by the monstrous current, and it was left to the three of us to run the rapid alone.

It was no small thing. Since it became a "Wild and Scenic River" fifty years ago, the river had taken thirty-nine lives, more than a few at the very spot we stood. The white water concealed a pothole, a tunnel that at high water would pull a body so deep into the rock it might never be recovered. We looked at the water. We looked at each other. To portage or to risk it? We weren't here to carry our boat. Still, the river looked like a different sort of animal, the kind you generally want to encounter behind a fence.

Then we saw something. Downstream, and just visible through the thick curtain of endless rain, stood the kayakers. On the prow of a rock stood one of my brothers, waving to us.

"He's waving us down," I said, and we all agreed, or at least decided not to disagree.

He wasn't, of course, though we wouldn't learn that until later. He was waving us off, telling us to walk around the Bull, to carry our boat, to drag our boat. To do anything short of attempting to ride the Bull. We must have known that on some level. I must have known that. But if I'd come to the river carrying this strange inertia, I must also have come believing the river could wash me of such. Stupid. Very stupid. Questions of the soul do not sit well next to questions of hydraulics.

Yet we walked back to our boat and strapped on our helmets. We were just about to push off when we saw him on the bank. We'd seen no one else all day, but on the opposite bank stood a figure, a man, waving us over.

"Who is that?" I asked, or someone did.

No one had an answer. No one said we should paddle over either, yet, for whatever reason, we did.

We banked close enough to see he was middle-aged but fit, wearing outdoor gear that even through the rain appeared antiquated: the Orvis vest, the canvas shorts. A bucket hat hung just above the brush of his mustache. Like us, he was soaked but smiling.

"You fellas running the Bull?" he asked.

We said we were, and he nodded thoughtfully.

"River's over five feet," he said. "Flood waters. Y'all ran it this high before?"

We hadn't and admitted as much.

"Well what would you fellas think of me hopping in?" he asked. "I've run it a time or two, and to be honest I need to get downriver."

"You've run it at this level?" I asked.

"I have," he said. "I've swam it too."

Though the raft was meant for three people, we made room, and the man took up residence in the back.

"When we drop in, we dig for the right bank," he said. "When I give the word fall into the boat, and boys, do hang on to your t-grips."

Though I've run the Bull any number of times, I've never lost the sensation of approaching it. It's fear, adrenaline. It's giving yourself over to some wild thing far more powerful than you, and far outside your control—something we don't do so often anymore in our well-managed lives. The feeling was immediately justified: As quick as we entered the current I felt it grab us with a force I'd never felt before. We flashed toward the first eddy, the point at which we'd dig for the right bank and slip around Decapitation Rock.

"Right back, right back!" the man called, signaling for the right side to back paddle. "Dig, fellas! Dig!"

We dug. Still, you could feel the boat being pulled off the line toward the pothole and whatever watery death lay beneath it.

"Dig!"

The raft began to pirouette, to run off the line not backward but at an angle, and for a moment I looked downriver and saw, or thought I saw, my brother on that rock, his arms in the air as if in supplication. We came to rest on the rock shelf perched above Decap. We'd completely missed the line and were now stuck on a sliver of rock. At any moment we'd come loose and plunge sideways into the pothole. Yet for one moment we were perfectly still. It was like being perched on the back of a great white shark.

You don't want to be there. Yet the only other place you can be is somewhere far worse.

That was when the man went to work. Before I even realized what was happening he had clipped a rope to the bow D ring and was out of the raft swimming—swimming!—against the current and toward the bank. When I raised up to see that he'd made it to the far side, the line between us now taut as a high wire, he waved me to sit down. He gave the rope a yank and then another and slowly, ever so slowly, I realized he was turning our raft back toward the line and away from the pothole.

"Get down, get down!" I yelled, and we did.

A moment later I felt the boat give way, felt it slip off the rock and slam into the current, turning perfectly into the rapid.

We washed through so fast it had no more occurred to me we were in the Bull before we were out of it, fifty, then a hundred feet downstream, dazed and drifting through the choppy water, the Bull receding in the rain, suddenly no more than a dull roar.

We paddled another hundred feet before we spotted my brother and the other kayakers on the bank. Even through the sound of the rain we could hear them, a mass of voices both panicked and exhilarated.

"You ran it! What the hell were you thinking! You ran it perfectly!"

My brother threw us a rope.

"Unbelievable," he said. "You guys ran it perfectly."

"Not exactly perfectly," I said.

We pulled ashore and told them about the man, about the pothole, about how he had swam—yes, swam—to the bank and pulled us back onto the proper line.

"That's not possible."

"I'm telling you," I said. "We saw it."

"We saw it too," my brother said, and with that he took out his phone and showed us the video. It was shot through the rain, but even from a distance it was evident we had run the line perfectly from start to finish, alone.

There was no one else in the boat.

There never was.

It would be years before I could track down the story of the Lost Guide and even when I did, the details were always a little different. But the story itself was always the same: How the man only appeared in the worst of weather conditions. How he guided boats through. How he was always dressed in the same outdated gear. How he had come to rest there, how almost fifty years prior to that day at the Bull the lost guide had dived into the water to pull a child from the pothole. How in saving the child's life he had lost his own, pulled into the pothole where they say you can hear the sound of water, yes, but also the faint echo of voices, a ghostly unsettling sound that now swims in my own head. A sound I hear on the wettest of nights, when the rain is falling and the fog is thick. The sound of moving water, the sound of moving time. The sound of what will eventually wash over us all, no matter what line we follow.

The Brown Mountain Lights

—ZACKARY VERNON—

My name is Mary Catherine Murphy. I'm not even Catholic, but somehow I ended up with the most Catholic name in history. My parents are Holy Rollers, sure, but not the Catholic kind. They go to this church called Fount of Life, one of those nondenominational numbers. But don't worry. This is in Raleigh. There's no snake handling or anything. Just your run of the mill buddy-buddy Jesus, the congregation in polos and Lilly Pulitzer, the band trying to make the whole thing seem cooler than it is. Our pastor wears flip-flops.

Anyway, I'm just saying this as we get to know one another. My pronouns are she/her.

Right. What brings me here today?

Well, I'm a junior, a psych major, but I'm taking this course called Intro to Folklore. I needed a "Humanities Experience" class, and folklore seemed less dumb than the other options. Don't get me wrong, I love the humanities. I've read *Where the Crawdads Sing*, like, twelve times. In high school I went through a tortured Sylvia Plath stage, and before that Harry Potter was my whole life. But since I got to App State I've been committed to the social sciences—the human mind, gender dynamics, class conflicts, all that stuff.

Now that Thanksgiving is over and finals week is right around the corner, my research paper is due soon for Intro to Folklore. Here's the syllabus. The assignment prompt is right there at the end. But let me back up first. My professor is Helen Shapiro. Supposedly she's a big deal in her field, gets boatloads of grants and awards.

Oh, you've taken a class with her. Then you know what we're dealing with here. I should say, she's fine, at least as far as humanities professors go. That's the thing they don't tell you when you sign up for Intro to Folklore. Dr. Shapiro is actually an English professor, precisely what I was trying to avoid. I thought folklore would be more like anthropology—you know, the lighter side of the social sciences.

On the first day of class, Dr. Shapiro was wearing a fringed leather jacket, like, leaning way too hard into the whole Daniel Boone thing or something. And in her lecture she went wild. I mean she was nearly frothing at the mouth as she gave us an overview of the field. "Folklore," she yelled, "is the study of all human belief, expression, and material culture," which makes it sound like the study of, well, everything.

Then Dr. Shapiro started pulling stuff out of a bag—an old jug with a face on it, a pipe that some bigwig smoked, a bow from a dead fiddler—and raving about how much we could learn from these things. "The stories!" she screamed. "Human history is nothing but stories!" That seemed pretty obvious. But she did go on to say something about whose stories get repeated and how that tells us everything about the nature of power in a society, which I guess could be interesting.

She lost me again when she started in on "object-oriented ontology." I can't even begin to explain that one. Sometimes I think people in the humanities try too hard.

Yes, back to the prompt. Basically, we have to choose an object or a traditional Appalachian belief and then write a research paper on it. You know how I feel about the ontology thing, so I chose the latter. Dr. Shapiro had a whole list of potential topics—farmers hanging dead snakes on fences to bring rain, hearing a screech owl foretelling the death of a loved one, et cetera. I chose the Brown Mountain Lights, figuring that story at least seemed kind of mysterious.

Wait, I forgot to mention—and this is the absolute worst thing of all—it's a group project. Dr. Shapiro picked our groups for us, and I got stuck with Todd and Autumn. They're dating, and yet somehow Shapiro thought it'd be okay to have them in the same group. Todd is an English major and has "Beauty is truth, truth beauty" tattooed on his forearm like an idiot. And Autumn is a theater major who uses about thirty-five different accents in a single conversation.

By the way, I haven't had a boyfriend since I got to App. I've been too focused on my schoolwork to even think about dating. So it was annoying to be stuck in a group with Todd and Autumn. They're sucking face all the time—in the library, in the cafeteria, even in class. As usual with group projects, I ended up doing all the work.

I started researching online first. Our teachers always tell us not to use Wikipedia, but I find stuff is true on there all the time.

The Brown Mountain Lights are, as you might guess, these weird, unexplainable lights that appear above Brown Mountain. It's not far from Boone, just about thirty miles south of here. Oh, good, you know about it.

There are all these theories floating around about what these lights are. One is that it's a slave.

You're so right! I meant *enslaved individual.* I usually have my Writing Center appointments with Chad. He's good at reminding me of things like that too.

Yes, this enslaved individual supposedly walks around the mountain with a lantern looking for his so-called "master." See, I put that in air quotes, so you know that's not me talking.

I'm not buying this theory, because what kind of enslaved individual would want to get back with his "master"? Have you seen *Django Unchained*? Tarantino's a misogynistic asshole, but I think he got some things right in that movie. Or at least that's how I imagine it, the desire for vengeance.

Some people claim that Brown Mountain was once the location of a war between the Cherokee and the Catawba, and others say all sorts of things about aliens. There was even an episode of *The X-Files* about it.

Some theories are less out there: ball lightning, natural gases, or fox fire, this eerie bioluminescent glow created by certain fungi in the forests.

All of these are either far-fetched or boring. I wanted a more scientific approach for our project. I looked up videos on YouTube and was shocked to find one that featured a professor from App. This guy's an astrophysicist, and he ... actually I don't know his pronouns. I should have asked. But they set up cameras on Brown Mountain and captured all kinds of lights. They concluded that 90 percent of the sightings had natural and human sources, things like lightning or car headlights bouncing off of clouds. The kicker is that I was sitting in this person's office, and after the spiel they gave about their research, I said, "So what about that last 10 percent? What are those lights?"

"We don't know," they said. "We can't explain it."

Well, that was a waste of time, I recall thinking. And then I remembered that my childhood doctor in Raleigh, Dr. Johnson, had actually turned into a huge alien enthusiast. He's losing patients these days, I heard, because he won't stop going on about UFOs, even in appointments. Someone comes in for tonsil pain, and they have to sit through a lecture on Roswell.

I called Dr. Johnson and asked if I could interview him over the phone for the project. He agreed immediately. These people crave attention. But I could barely get Dr. Johnson to talk about the Brown Mountain Lights. Instead, he kept going on and on about orbs. It was orbs this and orbs that. They're seen all over the world, according to him, and they reach incredible speeds and stop and hover and change directions in ways that no man-made object ever could.

Good catch. *Human*-made object.

Dr. Johnson said to look up all these different people—David Grusch, Chris Bledsoe, Steven Greer. I can't remember the others.

At one point, he could tell that I was skeptical, and he said, "The overlap in the Venn diagram between kooks and what the government has confirmed is much bigger than you would imagine."

The point, if Dr. Johnson ever got to anything close to a point, was that he believes the government has found alien technologies and probably reverse engineered them. That this knowledge has not been spread to the world, he says, is one of the greatest evils in human history. So many lives could be saved if we discovered a free source of energy, which I guess the orbs have.

With topics like this, you get to conspiratorial nuts in a jiffy, and they always want to say the government is either confirming or covering up the truth. I'm sick of it.

After Dr. Johnson, the only other option I had was to go to Brown Mountain myself. I told Dr. Shapiro about this, and she got all excited. She called it fieldwork.

So my group went out there, Todd and Autumn in the back of the old minivan my parents gave me when I came to App and me in the front like I was a chauffeur. We drove on the Blue Ridge Parkway and stopped at an overlook with a view of Brown Mountain. Other people were already there when we arrived. They had camping chairs and coolers set up everywhere. Some of them had on those glowing necklaces, and one guy was wearing a hat made of aluminum foil. Everyone whooped when we got out of the car. Some had clearly been drinking.

Pretty much right away, Todd and Autumn lay down on a blanket, looked up at the night sky, and started whispering and giggling. I got so mad I took off down a path that led away from the overlook. It was pitch-black dark. I turned on my cellphone's flashlight and kept going. If I saw them kiss one more time, I swear I was going to murder them. It got darker and darker the deeper I got into the valley. I thought about turning around a couple of times, but I worried Todd and Autumn would think I was scared. Also, I liked how quiet it was. So I just pressed on and on.

Then my cell phone cut off. It was fully charged. But it just went dark, and I couldn't see a thing. At that point I stopped being able to breathe. My mother used to say, "Mary Catherine's having a fit." But I'm a psych major now, and I know better. I was having a full-blown panic attack. The harder I tried to breathe the more impossible it became. I fell to my knees, sucking in and out desperately. I knew I'd never be able to walk out of that valley alone, not without a light. I was about to flop over on the ground when I saw through the rhododendrons the flicker of a fire. I pulled myself up and stumbled toward it.

I'm sorry. I'm actually a bit short of breath right now. No, no, I'll be fine. I was about to explain my hand. I'm sure you've been wondering about this big bandage. Not the most attractive thing, is it?

When I reached the fire, there was a man.

Is it hot in here?

He was sitting by the fire, and that was normal enough. He didn't seem weird at first. He was actually very handsome, tall and dark, and he was wearing a black suit, which I guess was a little weird for someone who was camping. But something else about him was scary, put me in mind of church for some reason.

He stood up and bowed like a gentleman. My panic attack was subsiding at this point, even despite the man. He waved his hand across the fire and said, "Sit a spell."

I swear to God there was not a chair there when I walked up. But it was there now, and something about it made me want to sit. It was like the chair had a gravity all its own.

I told him that my name was Mary Catherine and that I was a student at App. I don't know why, but I launched into the whole deal about Intro to Folklore and the Brown Mountain Lights. I couldn't stop talking. He listened and nodded. When I finished, we sat for a minute in silence. The fire crackled in front of us, and we both stared at it from our opposite sides.

Then he looked up at me, like directly at me. I could see the whites of his eyes, and the centers of them were black. He smiled, and I think his teeth were bleeding. I had to grab the sides of the chair to steady myself. This is gross, but I almost threw up. I tasted it in my mouth.

The man gestured around at the dark beyond our little circle of rhododendrons. "We've been here over a hundred years," he said, real slow and dramatic. "I was a barker, you see, at a traveling show. We were crossing this way, moving our little circus from Lenoir up to Boone. But we never made it, shouldn't have even been out this way. We were lost on account of a storm that came out of nowhere."

He paused as if concentrating on something. He wiped his sleeve across his mouth, and blood streaked his face.

"We tried to cross Wilson Creek. But when we had all our buggies on the bridge, the water rose up and swept us away. We struggled, but no one survived."

I asked, "Who? Who's *we*?"

"Them," he said, and all the sudden there were faces around us, poking out of the rhododendrons. I don't know how to describe them. I realize I'm breathing heavily right now. This will pass, though, I promise.

"My carnies," he said. "The pinhead, the alligator boy, the dwarf, the lobster girl, the limbless wonder, the impossibly fat woman."

I know. I can't stand fat-shaming either. So I said, "Whoa, don't be a dick!" He looked at me and shook his head in a confused way. I said, "Also, I don't know if *carnies* is politically correct."

"What does *politically correct* mean?" he asked like he was hearing it for the first time.

"It means that certain things are offensive. Like, um, everything you just said."

I smiled at the figures around us, but at the same time I was trying hard not to stare. They were moving closer. I felt them creeping in. They formed a circle around us and around the fire, and the circle kept getting smaller and smaller.

"So there you have it," the man said.

"Have what?" I was still mad at him for calling this lady fat. I looked over at her, and she was slowly peeling a banana.

He said, "There you have the story of the Brown Mountain Lights. The souls of carnies aren't like the souls of norms like you. We glow like orbs in the night sky, especially when we die in some tragic way."

I looked at him, and I guess my face seemed doubtful. "Cross my heart," he said.

In that moment, I remember thinking, *Dr. Shapiro will eat this up*. My GPA is a bit low at the moment. I had some trouble last year after my dog died. My mom didn't even tell me he was sick, and I—

Yes, let's get back on track. So I'm at the fire, and I pulled my phone out of my pocket. It was still dead. I asked him if I could come back and record him telling the story.

"Will you bring others?" he asked. Blood and spit were bubbling at the corner of his mouth.

"My partners Todd and Autumn, they'll come."

"Promise?" The people were so close now. I could have touched the lady. She was smiling and chewing loudly on her banana.

"Sure."

"Let's shake on it," he said.

Just as I was about to take his hand, I saw Todd and Autumn out of the corner of my eye. Autumn screamed, and I looked down. I wasn't shaking his hand. In fact, he had gone, and I'd stuck my hand directly into the fire.

God, look at how I'm shaking now. The burn is still pretty bad. I can't even write with this hand. I got one of those special passes that says I can take all my finals orally.

Only ten more minutes? Are you serious? And there aren't any more appointments available this week? No, don't bother putting me on a wait list. Let's just get down to the nitty-gritty.

I know I must sound insane, but all of this is true. I swear to God. And you can be confident about that because I'm not the kind of person who believes in ghosts. The field of psychology has disproven that sort of thing for decades. Seeing ghosts is merely a symptom of a disturbed mind.

What do I do now? I realize you can't write the paper for me. I'm very aware of what "falls within the purview of the Writing Center." I came here to sort things out. Todd and Autumn won't even talk to me since the incident. Autumn claims she looked into my eyes by the fire and says I was *possessed*. Can you believe that? Her with all those accents coming out a hundred miles an hour?

So this project falls on me now. I knew from the beginning that it would. Dr. Shapiro isn't going to give us an extension. Everybody knows what a hard-ass she is about these things.

I'm wrapping up, I promise. It all comes down to this: How do I write the paper knowing what I now know? Here's what Dr. Shapiro wants the thesis to be: The Brown Mountain lights aren't supernatural, but what people believe is real means more than what is actually real. That's pretty much the class in a nutshell.

But there's this other direction too. I could tell the truth—the *real* source of the lights. Damn the experts. Those carnies were there. I saw them right before I blacked out by the fire in the valley. Did I mention that? I woke up later that night in the Boone hospital. I was wearing one of those gowns with the back all open. Lying there in bed, I could still feel the pain in my hand from where I shook the barker's hand, even though it was all wrapped up in gauze and the nurse had clearly given me something that made my head feel like the inside of a conch shell.

Shit! Our time is up already?

The Sweetest Siren of the French Broad

—HEATHER BELL ADAMS—

When Sarah came out of dance class on Thursday, a man she'd never seen before was waiting on the sidewalk. Even though it was late May and plenty warm, he wore a scarf around his neck. He stared straight at her, and Sarah looked around, trying to figure out what had caught his attention, but the other girls were waving goodbye and climbing into their parents' cars. One after another, the car doors closed—slam, click, slam—leaving Sarah alone with the man. No sign of her mother anywhere. She hitched her backpack higher on her shoulder.

"Pretty evening, isn't it?" the man said. Besides the scarf—striped red and white like a candy cane—he had on a faded sweatshirt and black running pants. His hair was longer than Sarah's dad's. "What did you work on in class today?" His voice was so quiet she almost had to step closer to hear him, which of course she wouldn't do because she didn't want to encourage him. He nodded up toward the studio windows, which glowed like some kind of fierce warning in the last bit of sun. "Plié? Jeté? Arabesque?"

Sarah, who at eleven knew better than to talk to strangers, shook her head. Mrs. Polega was probably still upstairs in the studio, packing up the stretching bands and Bluetooth speaker. But the walls of the building were made of river stone, and who knew if Mrs. Polega could hear her if she screamed.

The man played with the ends of his scarf, revealing a mole shaped like Florida on the back of his hand. He took a step closer. When he lifted his hand to his ear, cupping it like he heard something interesting, Sarah felt icicles on her neck, like he'd tried to tickle her. She whipped around to look for help, and right then her mother showed up and Sarah jumped in the car as quickly as she could.

Her mother frowned as she checked the rearview mirror. "You okay? You're all flushed."

Sarah nodded. Maybe she should mention the strange man, but he'd disappeared, so what was the point? Her mother apologized for being late, muttering about having to scrape out a pot of burned lentils, and Sarah convinced herself she'd never see him again.

On Saturday Sarah's dad took her fishing. Their favorite spot was a tucked-away creek outside Horseshoe. Hardly anyone knew about it. Sarah liked this time the best, when the whole morning stretched out, and her dad, who always picked the best places along the bank, took his time helping her tie a lure to the end of her line. Unlike some of her friends' dads, Sarah's never raised his voice, not even when, whipping around in a wobbly pirouette in the formal dining room, she'd knocked her grandmother's—his mother's—punch bowl off the sideboard and it shattered into a million pieces. Even then he'd only bitten his lip and bent down to pick up what he could.

Now their lines bobbed, all chance and possibility, in the coffee-colored water. Along the edge of the creek honey-gold reeds swayed in a secret rhythm.

"Hey, Dad, do you think I could switch out of dance?" Sarah had asked before, a couple weeks ago, but she figured it didn't hurt to ask again. Dance had turned out to be boring.

Her dad kept his eyes on the water. "We could ask your mom, honey. She's the one who'll have to drive you. That choir you've been talking about is clear across town."

Sarah sighed. If she could join the choir, she could learn how to perform like a real concert singer, the sound rising up from between her stomach and chest. The whole family had been to a choir concert at Christmas, and the soloist's voice—a shard of crystal, a bell ringing out—had lingered in Sarah's teeth for three days.

"Maybe we can ask Mom again tonight?" Sunlight glittered on the creek, and in her mind she traced its path to the French Broad and then to the Mississippi. Out here by the water she wondered whether magic might be possible. The fairy tales in her book with the purple ribbon bookmark—ogres who lurked beneath bridges, horses that took off flying, thistles that when bitten whisked away sorrow—could be as real as the ham sandwiches her mother had packed for their lunch or the paper cut on Sarah's pointer finger.

Later, as they packed up the tackle box and cooler, footsteps sounded on the path. Sarah glanced up, expecting to see a hiker. Instead, she discovered the man from the dance studio, the same striped scarf around his neck. She shivered as she touched her own neck, remembering the fairy tale where a girl's head had fallen off. When the man looked right at her, Sarah darted behind her dad.

"You okay, pumpkin?" her dad asked.

Sarah stayed as still as possible. Her dad whipped around and said, "I got you," and her heart jumped, and she screamed. Her dad, who must have thought she'd been playing a game, dropped the tackle box and knelt in front of her. "Are you okay? You're shaking like a leaf."

"There was a man. Up there on the path." Sarah pointed, but the man was gone.

Her dad squeezed her shoulder as he stood. "Probably out for a walk in this nice weather."

Sarah had never been one to wake up with nightmares, never bothered her mom or dad crying about a boogeyman in the closet or a spider under the bed. She was much too grown-up to turn silly now. At home she kept her desk neat and her spiral notebooks arranged in rainbow order. Lately, she'd been working on her plan for when she grew up. The other day at school her teacher had said, "Why, Sarah, someday you'll travel the world, mark my words." Right then and there Sarah had decided she would do exactly that. Bridget wanted to wear high heels and work in an office with a glass desk, and Chelsea talked about owning a store that sold aquariums and terrariums. Sarah hadn't known what she wanted until she heard the idea of going to different countries. In art class, she'd sketched a map, tracing an imaginary journey all the way from the mountains of western North Carolina to the pyramids in Egypt. Before the bell rang, she'd added a stick figure beneath the tallest pyramid, her hand raised in a wave and a wide-brimmed hat on her head because her mother always worried about her getting sunburned.

After they got home from fishing, Sarah's dad unpacked the fish they'd caught and handed them to her mother, who flicked on the faucet at the outdoor sink.

Sarah sat on the porch floor with her knees drawn up to her chest. "I've seen that man before." She couldn't explain the fear still pooling in her chest. In the undergrowth around the porch, cicadas screeched, panicked.

Her father frowned. "The man from the creek? Where have you seen him?"

"After dance."

"What man are you talking about? One of the fathers?" her mother asked.

Her dad snapped the cooler shut. "Has he tried to talk to you?"

"He asked what I'd done in class."

Her mother unsheathed her knife. "Stay close by your friends and you'll be fine. Try not to worry about it." She chopped off a fish head and scraped it down the drainboard into a bucket.

"If he's hanging around again, and we can't figure out who he is, let's say something to somebody," her dad added.

Sarah nodded. The man would have no reason to be interested in her. Moriah had the best hair, and Chelsea already wore a training bra. Why would he look Sarah's way? Her knees were covered with scabs, and she wasn't even allowed to wear tinted lip gloss.

But still she wondered if the man could be huddled in the trees beyond the porch. This very minute he might be out there rubbing the mole on his hand, his eyes glowing in the dark.

At bedtime, Sarah was suddenly scared of being alone in her room, where shadows she'd never noticed before crept across the ceiling. Despite the heat, she pulled the covers up to her chin. Like always, at least in the spring and summer, her window was open a few inches. Her mother said air-conditioning pumped dangerous chemicals into your lungs.

A bug batted against the screen, and Sarah jumped. From outside, a different sound, a rustling, the crunch of pine needles. Her ears strained, and she opened her eyes as wide as possible like that might help her hear better. Another crunch, then another, maybe footsteps slowly crossing the yard.

Sarah sat up in bed. She could call for her mom or dad, but they'd already told her not to worry. In the shadowy dark, her desk and dresser loomed larger than in the daytime. The walk to her bedroom door stretched as long as a football field, the safety of the dimly lit hallway as distant as outer space. Under the covers her legs trembled.

Outside an owl called, and she gasped and squeezed her eyes shut. By the time she opened them again a shadow had appeared at the window. Was it her imagination or did the window—slowly, quietly—open another inch? Sarah held her breath and willed the window to stay still. The shadow behind it grew larger.

Something or someone pushed the window up and yanked the screen away. A body squeezed through and landed on her floor. Everything sped up. Sarah opened her mouth to scream, but the figure, the man, stood and lunged toward her bed and held a washcloth against her face so she could only grunt and flick her tongue against the cloth. It smelled like medicine or licorice. He flung her over his shoulder. She kicked and hit as hard as she could, but the washcloth had made her dizzy and weak. He pushed her out of the window, and before she could try to stand, he climbed out and scooped her back up. It started to rain, the night sky crying purple-dark and bats shadowing against the moon.

When Sarah forced her eyes open, she found the man crouched in front of her, staring. His own eyes were bloodshot. He reached for her, and she whimpered, but he slipped off the washcloth and tossed it aside. His fingers smelled like night crawlers and grubs. Hoping she'd fallen into a nightmare, she blinked and tried to wake up. They were in some kind of storage shed where the only light came from a lantern on the concrete floor. When she pinched the tender skin at her wrist, it stung, which told her she wasn't asleep.

"Can I have a drink of water?" Sarah tried to sit, but he'd tied her hands and feet with rope, and it took some rocking back and forth to make her way up.

The man sighed as he stood and rummaged in a cooler. Her breath coming short and fast, Sarah searched for whatever clues she could uncover. The shed was cluttered with junk—stacks of yellowed newspapers, rusted coffee cans overflowing with nails, a twelve-pack of store-brand soda. A horrible sadness clung to the place. She noticed a Zebco spincast in the corner and a pack of moss-green fishing line.

He turned back. His shoulders sagged like he carried some heavy, invisible thing. The wind moaned a frightened tune, rattling the door to the shed. *Help, help.*

"I had a daughter once," the man said, his voice gravelly and angry as he squatted in front of her. "Her mother took her away." He gave Sarah a plastic cup, and, her hands still bound together, she tipped it to her mouth. Dank, warm water, nothing but a trickle. Though it tasted of rotten leaves, of river mud, of tragedy, she swallowed and wished for more.

She didn't ask about his daughter because she had a bad feeling nothing good had happened to her. Or maybe, after the mother took her away, the man never saw her again.

"Who are you?" Sarah asked.

He grabbed the cup back. The mole on his hand was darker than she'd remembered, and it pulsed a jagged beat so that she wondered if he felt his heartbeat in it.

He put his hand to his ear, the same way he'd done before and screwed up his mouth like he was sucking on a pebble. "You hear that?"

Sarah shook her head. The lantern made a faint ticking sound. If only she could spirit herself back home and into her bed. Weeks ago, before the man showed up, Moriah had asked her what superpower she would pick, and Sarah said she wanted to imagine a place and go there, magically, without a car or plane, just *poof*, all of a sudden you're in a grass hut cracking open a coconut or on top of Mount Everest wearing lace-up boots caked with muddy snow.

"That's not a real superpower," Moriah had said, shoving a stick of cinnamon gum in her mouth. "I'd want to read people's minds."

But if Sarah were asked again, her answer would be the same. She didn't care to know what thoughts swam through the man's mind. She'd rather wish herself back to her feather pillow, the notebooks lined up on her desk, the uneven chorus of her mom and dad snoring down the hall.

The man hummed, closing his eyes and swaying. "There's this frequency, a vibration, I don't know. It's almost like you're singing a song only I can hear." He frowned. "I can't quite make it out though. You're not actually singing, are you?" He opened his eyes. This time he glared at her, like she'd disappointed him.

Sarah shivered. The water she'd swallowed soured in her stomach. Every week before class the girls at the dance studio gossiped. Who got a 60 on the spelling quiz, who smelled like BO, who stuffed paper towels in a sink in the second-floor girls' bathroom and turned the water on full blast until a river flowed under the swinging door. Sarah had never been the subject of any of the talk. She'd never wanted to be. Even now, with the man's eyes drilling into her, she worried what story she might be part of and what would be said about her.

The man reached forward, and Sarah thought briefly, hopefully, he would untie the ropes and let her go. He repeated what he'd said before, about her singing. Up close his breath smelled like coffee. His eyes were a watered-down green, like pond scum.

She started to shake all over. "Please, let me go." Maybe she could find a way to escape. Sarah's dad always told her she could do anything if she tried her hardest. The man leaned closer, stroking the scarf until, suddenly, terribly, he looped it around her neck.

Ever since her grandmother's funeral, Sarah had asked her parents, her dad especially, where people went when they died. Their answers depended on their mood. Sometimes they said heaven, and when she asked for details, they talked about streets paved with gold and angels in robes.

"Choir robes?" Sarah asked. "Are they singing angels?"

Other times they said a quiet place or a garden. Once Sarah's mother was bringing in the laundry from the clothesline, and she sighed and said, "Nowhere. They lay there and try to sleep." Sarah didn't like this answer because she imagined her grandmother smothered with dirt.

Sarah opened her eyes to find herself underwater. Strangely calm, she wondered about the name of this murky place with its distant music of frogs and bird chatter. The next time she woke up, she was startled to discover a group of women surrounding her. In a foggy haze she counted them, landing on six. Their flowing hair glimmered in the morning sun. They floated and swam and danced, all by barely fluttering their birdlike legs. Meanwhile the scabs on Sarah's own legs had mysteriously healed.

"Where am I? Am I dead?" Water rushed into Sarah's mouth, and she swallowed it without thinking. Instead of choking, she felt herself grow stronger.

"The French Broad," one of the women said. Her face begged to be looked at—violet eyes, aqua glitter on her eyelids, a mouth like a flower.

Another swam over. "You'll miss your family and friends at

first, but I promise you'll learn to be happy here. We have so little cares, so few worries. I won't say it's better than your life before, but you'll see."

"All will be explained," another said knowingly.

Time had no meaning on the river, and Sarah couldn't tell whether days or weeks had passed. Beneath the dandelion-yellow sun she floated, trying not to think of home.

One day the woman with the violet eyes said Sarah could begin her lessons.

"What kind of lessons? What do you mean?" Sarah asked. They were lounging on a sandbar in the middle of the river. Turtles lined the banks sunning themselves.

"Why, singing, of course." The woman's laugh sounded like wind chimes. "Don't you know we're sirens?" She ran her fingers through the tangles in Sarah's hair. "We've needed your dulcet childish tone to become even more powerful."

Sarah shivered at how creepy this sounded. Maybe she belonged here, and maybe she didn't.

Another siren swam up. "You'll be the sweetest siren of the French Broad. Tell me, lovely, are you sad? You're not sad, are you?"

"Just the tiniest bit." Sarah missed her parents a lot and her friends a little, but the river's current spirited away the worst of the hurt.

The not-quite-mothers taught her breathing, pitch, and rhythm. Once in a while, in the mornings, the very best time for fishing, Sarah thought of the man who had snatched her from her bed, and anger sparked at the back of her throat. Still, what could she do? Her new life was easy, but pointless. Sometimes she felt trapped. It seemed a long time ago, ages and ages, that she'd wanted to travel the world.

"One day you'll face a challenge you must conquer alone, and you will grow stronger from the effort," the sirens told her, urging her to be patient.

Every day Sarah practiced singing, melodies that drifted over the river like satin ribbons. One fall morning near the end of trout season, the man showed up, almost like he'd been summoned. The other sirens hummed their encouragement and swam away, leaving Sarah alone in the middle of the river. She shook all over with fear and the first whispers of understanding.

Reel it in nice and slow, her dad used to say. She slipped off the sandbar. The river's current, gentle but insistent, nudged her toward the muddy banks where the man who'd taken her stood watching. He carried the fishing rod she'd noticed in his shed. Around him the woods burned with fall color, a riotous rage. Squirrels skittered in the branches above. Leaves crunched beneath his feet as he stepped closer. Twigs snapped. When Sarah noticed the striped scarf around his neck, she became paralyzed. She couldn't move or even think.

But magic danced along the river, the kind that swallowed bad memories. Sarah's dad had taught her about lures, and the sirens had shown her the rest. Now that she had the man's attention, she swam to a haunted place in the river where the sharpest rocks hid beneath the surface and vengeance churned, and she began to sing a song only he could hear.

The Raven Mockers

—ANNETTE SAUNOOKE CLAPSADDLE—

"Of owls who portend death and buzzards who carved life into these Smoky Mountains, no bird of prey has earned quite so *foul* a reputation, as the raven—or rather its giant mimic, the Raven Mocker."

"Dude. You really gonna lead with a pun?"

As he blinked from the stage into the audience seeking the origin of the comment, Jynx Wildcatt decided middle schoolers were becoming more and more jaded, almost as bad as high schoolers. High schoolers were most definitely the worst. Jynx had stopped doing Native American Heritage Month gigs for them in 2017 after some sophomore in Carhartt overhauls propped his Danner boots on the back of a front-row seat and shouted, "Go home," just after Jynx had finished the story of how Water Spider brought fire to the world. And then some girl in full Goth attire, fishnets and all, intervened by screaming back to the boy, "You first!" The whole assembly had been shut down. That day Jynx went home without a paycheck and had to call the school's secretary for the next three weeks before the district finally agreed to issue the full agreed-upon amount. High schoolers were also the reason he stopped wearing a breechcloth and leggings. Coverage be damned, teenagers just couldn't handle the possibility of catching a glimpse of forbidden skin. After only a couple of shows, Jynx had sewn himself some makeshift leather britches (to hell with authenticity) and simply requested the air-conditioning be cranked up whenever possible.

So with the threat of another show-stopping interruption and the end to his middle-school circuit for good, Jynx ignored this prepubescent's comment and skipped to the gory bits of the story quickly, before anyone else felt the need to chime in.

Sweat pooled between his toes, making the inside of his deerskin moccasins slick. It was time to pull out his most solemn, deepest performance voice. "Raven Mockers, in their truest form, are of a fiery shape, with ebony wings outstretched as they swoop down toward their targets." The bright red ribbons on Jynx's white cotton trade shirt rose and fell as he simulated flight. "They can mimic the common man or woman, though these beasts are withered from the worn lives they have ingested. Taking human life sustains them but does not make them youthful in appearance like other creatures you might hear about, such as vampires."

Jynx stepped to the front of the stage and leaned toward the audience. "The Raven Mockers' humanly appearance makes them especially dangerous because the common person cannot recognize them for the menace that they are. With sparks trailing their flight path, they seek out the dying, smell the ominous scents of death, and dive in to steal what little essence is left. They come like great storms—like gusts of wind and lightning, some say. Only the strongest of medicine men can ward them off." Jynx raised his chin so that he was almost blinded by the stage lights and crossed his arms tightly against his chest.

"Or medicine women?" A mousey-looking young woman from the front row shouted back. She looked familiar to Jynx. Maybe he remembered her from last year's assembly.

He nodded, blinking. "Sure. Medicine person." He didn't care. He just needed to get paid and get out of there.

Jynx refocused, a trick he learned long ago. He kept his eye trained on the back row of auditorium seats where the pretty Spanish teacher sat. She was a nice white lady who always offered to escort him on his visits as if he had never been to the school before, as if he hadn't attended that school for two years until he turned thirteen, before leaving to live with his dad in Charlotte. He liked to watch her nod when he said the word *balance* and could tell she wanted to touch his hair—she was one of those. But she had read enough blog posts that she just made jokes about people who asked to do it instead.

Jynx earned the bulk of his income in November, which helped make him the favorite uncle at Christmas when he returned to visit family in Charlotte, so he couldn't afford for any of these gigs to go wrong. Word travels fast in the school assembly/rest home circles. And it was easy money. He had tried working for the tribal government, the regular 7:45–4:30 office life. It wasn't bad. But it wasn't for Jynx either.

This Spanish teacher was nodding and smiling. He liked how she had one tiny dimple on her right cheek.

The rest of the gig went as expected, including pretty Señorita Smith leading him the long way from the stage to his vehicle in the parking lot. Jynx had wanted to stop off at the men's room to change out of his performance clothes, but he knew that would break some fourth wall for his escort, and he was nothing if not the consummate entertainer.

Jynx sat behind the steering wheel of his Dodge Grand Caravan minivan and watched as she waved adios from the school's double doors. He cranked the van and shook his head, a sly smile spreading across his face. *I still got it*, he assured himself. As he lifted his eyes to check his rearview, something perched on the powerline in front of him caught his attention. He blinked. Stage makeup had mixed with sweat and matted into the corners of his eyes. *Is that a* . . .

It was. It was a rather large owl. Midday, it perched motionless on the school's powerline. Jynx's heart grew large and heavy. *Death*, he thought. *Owls are omens of death.* He simply hoped it wasn't foretelling his.

Jynx put the van in reverse and headed toward Highway 74. As he drove, he considered how other Cherokees might argue with him about this omen of sorts. How some would say that it had to be a specific kind of owl and how, in truth, he wasn't an ornithologist even though he was Native and most white people expected him to be. But owls, all of them, always freaked him out. It would be best if he just drove straight home, especially since he hadn't even had a chance to change his clothes. He could heat up some hot dogs for dinner and do the grocery shopping the next day.

But the sky was a bright winter-day blue and so he turned off 74 and took the back road home. River cranes dotted the Oconaluftee. Groundhogs played dodgeball with his car and squirrels, ill prepared for winter's required stockpiles, attempted mass suicide. Jynx spoke to each varmint. Cursed a couple. His most recent paycheck rested in its envelope on the passenger seat, and he considered turning back toward town to deposit it, but as he flipped the blinker, he felt a jolt. And then another.

A flat. Jynx pulled onto the shoulder and put the car in park. No use looking for a spare. The van was used. Never came with one. He pulled out his cell phone from his gym bag.

He texted his buddy Fred, knowing good and well he was at work at the casino and would not answer his phone.

Gotta flat. Few miles from home. You free?

Jynx waited. He pressed his words on the screen. Tapped, *Send as text message*. He checked for signal bars. There was one, but that didn't mean much. No use calling anyone else.

There's benefit to living in these mountains most of one's life. You know what's just over the ridge. He hadn't planned on climbing a damn mountain that day, but he had planned even less on paying for a tow or calling an ex-girlfriend. Jynx was still in his performance regalia. Luckily, he had his gym bag of clothes with him, so he slid into the back of the van and pulled on a pair of gray sweat pants, an old Dallas Cowboys Super Bowl Championship t-shirt, and a pair of Air Jordans he wore that one year he thought he'd play point guard in the Senior Games, pulled a hammy during warm-ups of their first game, and never stepped on the court again. Jynx packed away his leathers and locked the van. It was a fine afternoon for a hike.

The leaves were thick and soft, causing him to slide most of the way up the bank from the asphalt until he could reach the old logging road he planned to take, winding around up and over the mountain. Once on the other side, he would be able to follow the river road about a mile to his house and be home before it got too dark.

At least that was what he remembered being able to do when he was a boy—when he and his cousins had no car, no driver's licenses, and all the time in the world as long as they got home before supper.

Not thirty minutes into his hike, he began to question his memory—just as a stone structure, one so weathered it was surely older than him, peeked out from the maples, buckeyes, and white ash.

A tendril of smoke ascended from the chimney of this stone cabin, dissolving into the growing chill of the afternoon. Jynx had never seen a place like this. There was no road fit for a car, no driveway leading to it. Even hunting camps had paths maintained well enough for ATVs to access. He scanned the area for signs of a grow site or other illegal manufacturing but couldn't even find a garden plot. No shed. No garage. Just this stack of stone and mud topped with a rusting tin roof. Jynx had heard tales of mountain men or women who shirked off life and resigned themselves to the woods. They became hermits, for all intents and purposes, but they usually at least maintained gardens.

Even more troubling, despite the chimney smoke, there was no vehicle of any sort. Jynx couldn't bum a ride. He surmised that whoever lived there had probably left not long ago. Jynx checked his phone again. No text from Fred. Still one bar. He wondered if the person inside had a landline. People who lived in places like this often kept one since the cell service wasn't reliable.

Jynx knocked on the door. He ran his hands across his forehead and smoothed down the wayward hairs that had pulled loose from his braids. He knocked again. He tried the doorknob. It turned. It clicked. The door's pressure gave, and Jynx almost stumbled inside with its release.

"'Ello! Anyone home? 'Ello?"

The cabin was dark, and his calls were met with silence. Jynx took a step inside and listened. There were no sounds of humans, but even more unsettling, there were no sounds of machines. No air-vent woosh. No refrigerator hum. No buzz of even a lamp left on for security. The only sound was that of a dying fire—the cracking and popping of burning wood. The hiss of flames seeking exit.

Jynx ran his hand along the walls, searching for a light switch but could not find one, so he walked in the direction of the fireplace as his eyes adjusted to the cabin's dimness. He could make out a kitchen table, he thought, but little else. *Where the hell would a phone be*? It appeared that the cabin was no larger than one room, so he placed his hand along one wall and began to walk. The coolness of the rock guided his palms, and he found it odd that no furniture caused him to stumble. He drew nearer and nearer to the fire, the warmth blushing his cheeks. *Where the hell—*

The door flung open behind him, lighting the room in a red

glow and vibrating the stone walls with a wailing cry like a goat bleating for its lost mother. Two large, winged shadows swooped into the room, sending dust particles dancing. Having bent to fit through the doorframe, they now straightened their torsos and shook their bodies right.

Jynx dove into a corner and hunkered onto his knees.

There was a clawing on the tin roof. From pitch to gutter, Jynx could hear a muffled cry that dug into his skin as deep as what he could only assume were the talons of some large bird of prey piercing the metal of the roof above. He closed his eyes, desperate to dull all his senses.

An earsplitting screech echoed in the chimney, and one more creature dropped down into the hearth and spilled out into the cabin, forcing Jynx's full attention again. With wide eyes, he expected to see a cauldron of bats or even a wayward raccoon.

Instead another human form emerged,, and now before Jynx there clearly appeared three pairs of burning eyes, deeply set into the bodies of two aged men-beasts and one elderly woman-beast, all hunched at the shoulders as if worn down by years or wings that now seemed to disappear into their shoulder blades. They stood on gnarled, sinewy legs like dried jerky and their arms hung loosely, far too close to the dusty floorboards of the cabin to make anatomic logic.

The three faced each other making a triangle of sorts, their backs to Jynx. He pushed himself deeper into the corner and tried to still his breath. He strained to keep his eyes on them, and still scan the fireplace to make sense of what he had seen of the third's arrival.

"I told you we should have gotten there earlier," the woman said and coughed as if to clear away the gravel from her throat. "But Pete just had to make a couple of stops first."

"Why not make the most of a trip, I always say." The smallest of the three, the one seemingly emerging from the fireplace, shook his shoulders. "That boy wouldn't have made it up from the river if—"

"If there hadn't been anyone there? That's what you always miss! You never look first. You lead with your nose, not your eyes," the largest of the beasts growled.

The one called Pete dropped his head. "No one noticed *us* either."

"Yes, but that wasn't the case at the old man's home, was it? Your delay almost got us killed. You flew us straight into medicine," the woman gurgled.

"No harm. No foul." He raised his head and stepped toward her in defiance.

Jynx's back straightened.

"Brother. Enough." The larger one stepped between them.

"Wait. Shhh." Pete tilted his chin to the ceiling, silhouetting a long, pointed nose. "Did either of you bring something home with you?"

"Like what?" the older brother asked.

Pete stepped back from the group and eyed the ground. He counted the marks in the dust. He followed their traces. "We aren't alone." He slammed the cabin door shut.

Jynx pushed his palm against his chest as if to check that his physical body was matching the fears of his mind. *Could these really be Mockers?* As the three creatures paced the room, Jynx ran through the logical questions. *Had he manifested them with his storytelling just hours before? Was the darkness playing tricks? Had he trained his brain to think this way?* It didn't matter. Jynx knew he was trespassing and these three did not appear kind nor forgiving. And regardless, how hard Jynx tried to reason through what he had seen, the smallest of the three had not entered through the door with the other two, and yet there he stood.

If Jynx was right about the Mocker stories, he would at least not allow them to take his heart. They couldn't. It wasn't his time. He might actually have a fighting chance if they were, in fact, not humans.

Jynx stood from his crouch and bolted past the group, praying he had memorized where the door was in darkness.

He heard a chorus of desperate squawks as he pushed past the threesome. He missed the door handle with his first grasp but managed to find it with his next. He flung the heavy wooden door open and bolted into the woods.

In the light of the forest, Jynx fumbled through the branches until he found a course that he felt not only led away from the cabin but toward his home. The forest came alive overhead with the calls of all fliers. Crows and woodpeckers. Squirrels and chipmunks. Songbirds, scavengers, and soaring rodents. Jynx tried to recall who might help him in his retreat, but he never told those stories onstage and had long forgotten them. He figured his best bet was just to keep moving. He was no dying man. He may have angered the Raven Mockers, but they would not be justified in taking his heart.

However, on the off chance these were merely humans distorted by darkness and fear, all bets were off. He needed to keep running.

Jynx crested the summit and fumbled his way down the mountain, weaving between rhododendron thickets until the treescape began to open up overhead. Brown wintertime kudzu rose so thick, Jynx couldn't see in front of him. He knew he must be close because kudzu only grew on banks near newly built roads. He bounded into the undergrowth on his hands and knees. He tore through vines, eager to keep a low profile now, so close to civilization. He could hear the rush of cars and river below.

For a moment, he paused, disoriented from the lack of sightline. He craned his neck to see above the kudzu but felt his shoulders being pulled downward. The plant moved as if no longer winter-dormant. It was growing up his shins and around his knees, pulling him down until all he could see were its brown, woody vines. There was a piercing pain in his gut. It was growing into him. Jynx reached to pull the vines away and felt a warm wetness.

Suddenly his arms were jerked forward and stretched over his head. He was being held upright and snatched toward the sky. Blood dripped from his fingers. Just as abruptly, he was dropped to the earth, onto his stomach, and felt his ankles clamped tightly by claws. Jynx turned to find his legs being pulled back through the creepers up the hill by black arms.

"But I am not dying!" he shouted.

Red eyes stared back. "We caught your last performance," he heard her say. "Yes, you are." She smiled at him, revealing a small dimple on her right cheek.

Little Betsy

—ROSS WHITE—

A ghost is no good to a child.
Maybe he crooks a finger, as if to beckon
the girl to play. Maybe he bounds spritely
down corridors, into kitchens.
But if she hands him a dolly or ball
and he reaches with his spectral hand,
he cannot clutch the gift, and if his failed grasp
surprises him, if the lack of resistance—
for everything real resists the touch—
unbalances him, his incorporeal fingers
might graze the child's offering hand.
What would you call the gooseflesh
raised by the frolicsome dead?
There is no joy in it, only a deep well
of longing cold, the kind that claws
through every crack in the wall.

How to Banish a Ghost

—ROSS WHITE—

Ask him gently, with a single candle
burning in the north end of the room, to
come back only when he is at peace.
Dismiss him with a stern prayer.
Eliminate all traces of him—bone, clothing,
furniture, the scent of him left in bedsheets.
Gesture with an upturned palm,
hiding in your other hand a key.
Inscribe on the frontispieces of his favorite books
joyful messages and give them to
kin who never met him.
Leave a lamp lit for two hundred days.
Mend the broken fence, the torn sole.
No ghost wants to stay a century
or watch his loved ones age and die.
Perhaps he cannot release a temporary
quarrel, one you can help him
resolve: dispute about the silver in a place
setting or custody battle for grandmother's
thimble. Perhaps a pocket watch was lost
under the porch and he must see it returned, or
violence was done to him
while he had a message to deliver.
Explain that he can will himself to visit
yesterday. Ask him to divide by
zero until he fades from view.

A House of Vine and Shadow

CONCLUSION: DOGWOOD

When Nate Batts was a boy, his family liked to drive all over the state, east and west, just for the fun, just to see. When he was a boy, he'd climbed Jockey's Ridge and Grandfather Mountain both, rode down the Blue Ridge Parkway and Highway 12 and almost all of Highway 64, he remembered, almost, not quite but close, so very close...

The old woman smiled at him, was smiling, had been smiling all this time, and Nate felt himself a-tremble, saw the iced tea slosh in its jar, felt its first spilled drops fall sticky on his hand.

But it was the old man who spoke. "Nice to know some parts of the place are still a little weird."

Nate thought, Nate struggled to say, *Some parts!?!? A little weird?!?!* But he could hear no sound come from his lips, and he could feel them move no more than to quiver.

"Nice to know some hollers still holler, some hills is trying still to kill the Devil even if Kill Devil Hills ain't," the old man said. "The Land of the Longleaf Pine, whose first colony was lost, whose easternmost shore is the Atlantic's graveyard, whose heart is where the Devil tramps, whose fortune was made by a crop that don't feed nor clothe but burns and kills. Nice to know there's some folks here who still might can read Armageddon in the weather."

"Foot," the old woman said, "whole place ain't nothing but a lie, anyhow, lines drawn on English parchments, paying no mind to Neuse nor Cape Fear, Watauga nor Dan."

"Oh, but what a lovely lie it's been sometimes."

"Has it? Done brought us to here."

"Think he's heard enough now?"

"I believe so. He's begun to take root."

Nate wanted to jump then because he felt what he was sure was a snake winding itself up his calf. He wanted to leap up out of the wingback chair, to rise up yelping, but he couldn't. He strained his thighs trying to stand, trying to kick, but he was bound, stuck, buried. With terrible work he managed at least to look down and saw twisting up his calves not a snake but vines, vines like the ones he'd seen outside the house, scuppernong and honeysuckle, cherry and strawberry and ivy, Virginia creeper and kudzu too all climbing and claiming him an inch at a time. Then he saw below the vines, saw not his feet nor his Tecovas but gray scales, almost like a lizard's but knottier, bumpier, and at last he gasped as he realized it was dogwood bark, dogwood bark grown over his feet, dogwood bark deep rooted in the muck below the floorboards.

No, Nate thought. *No. No.*

"No," he rasped, forcing out what little voice was left him. With all his strength he strained until he began to quiver, and when his strength was gone, he quivered with desperate panic until he began to shake his head.

"No!" he hollered.

He dropped the jar of iced tea.

The old woman frowned.

"Oh, foot," she said.

With a wild fury, a frantic urge for survival that his forebears had done all in their power, sinned horrible sins, to spare him, Nate Batts began to twist a near spasm until at last he could move his arms, and then he tore at the vines that twined his legs and the bark that scaled his feet. From one small corner of his eye he saw the old man's hand begin to reach, to come across the room toward him though the man did not rise from his seat. Nate thrashed his whole body side to side and then up, up, up, until at last he threw himself from the wingback chair. He stumbled, plunging more than running out of the parlor. He flung himself at the door, the door he'd half-expected to crumble when first he'd knocked what now seemed days ago.

The door gave to Nate's weight, and he felt himself falling, tumbling down, down…

Nate opened his eyes to the shining sun. He didn't know if he'd been unconscious or asleep or only out of his mind, if he'd lain a few seconds or days. He could hear singing birds. He could hear humming engines. He could feel himself bruised, his skin scraped, and then he realized he was laying on snow-white concrete. He raised his head enough to look around.

It was built, built all around him: the development his bosses intended. Overlarge houses as far as Nate could see, hectic gables and peaks without need or reason, gaping facades without balance or symmetry or beauty. They shone like plastic in the sun, surrounded by their moats of browning Bermuda grass.

Nate raised himself some more, enough to turn and look with rising fear behind him.

The old farmhouse, the house of vine and shadow, was gone. Another overlarge house, just like all the others, stood in its place. Six brick stairs rose to its front door, set in the middle of a stoop too narrow to sit on. Nate lay on the sidewalk that ran from the steps to the cul-de-sac. Behind the sidelight windows he could see the outline of a woman not much older than him, talking on her phone. He could see the raw concern in her eyes. He could see the concern was not for him.

As if climbing the scentless air he stood, feeling bruises and scrapes from his head to his toes, but at least he neither felt nor saw any dogwood bark. He decided he'd worry where his truck was come the morning. He took out his phone to call a ride, but it was dead, a black brick lifeless in his palm. He decided he'd worry about that when he was home.

To the west the sun was reddening. To the east the city's light began to glow, to glisten and bauble the evening sky above. In the house of vine and shadow he'd been afraid, over and over, until at last he'd feared for his life or at least his soul. Here, though, now, where the house of vine and shadow stood no more, in this scape of sham and silence, he felt his blood and marrow chilled. He breathed deep once for air. He breathed deep again for scents but found none, no live oak, no pine, no laurel or chestnut. He listened but heard no birds for they had no place here to nest. He had to get out of this development, this venture, this colony he'd helped to create. Aways off, above the Bradford pears and the ugly peaks and gables, he could see pines still swaying, still standing. He turned and took a step.

Some flesh exploded cold and wet beneath his heel.

As if defusing a bomb he took off his boot and upended it over his hand.

Out fell a single, squashed scuppernong grape.

Contributors

A lifelong North Carolinian, **Heather Bell Adams** is the author of *Maranatha Road* (West Virginia University Press, 2017), *The Good Luck Stone* (Haywire Books, 2020), and *Starring Marilyn Monroe as Herself* (forthcoming Regal House). Her short stories appear in *New Letters*, *North Carolina Literary Review*, *The Thomas Wolfe Review*, *Broad River Review*, *Orange Blossom Review*, *Reckon Review*, and elsewhere. She was North Carolina's 2022 Piedmont Laureate.

Michele Tracy Berger is the Eric and Jane Nord Family Professor in Religious Studies, Professor of English Studies, and director of the Baker-Nord Center for the Humanities at Case Western Reserve University in Cleveland, Ohio. She is the author of the science fiction novella *Reenu-You* and of the story collection *Doll Seed*, whose title story, published in *FIYAH: Magazine of Black Speculative Fiction,* received the 2019 Carl Brandon Kindred Award.

Wiley Cash is the *New York Times* bestselling author of four novels and a 2025 recipient of the North Carolina Award for Literature. **Early Cash** is a fifth grader whose work has appeared in *Our State Magazine*, and she is currently at work on a novel. **Juniper Cash** is a fourth grader who enjoys making movies, running, and writing.

Annette Saunooke Clapsaddle is the author of *Even As We Breathe* (UPK, 2020), the first novel published by an enrolled citizen of the Eastern Band of Cherokee. The novel was a finalist for the Weatherford Award, winner of the 2021 Thomas Wolfe Memorial Literary Award, and named one of NPR's Best Books of 2020. Clapsaddle's work has appeared in numerous publications, including *The Atlantic*, *Salvation South*, *Bon Appétit*, and *Travel + Leisure*. She is the founder of *Confluence: An Indigenous Writers Workshop Series.*

Born in Lumberton, North Carolina, **Synora Hunt Cummings** grew up and currently resides in Johnston County, North Carolina, with her husband, three children, and English Bulldog. Cummings is an enrolled member of the Lumbee Tribe of North Carolina. She enjoys working with adolescents and youth and volunteering in her Native community. When she is not busy serving others, she enjoys baking elaborate cakes, back porch sitting, and traveling with her family.

Tyree Daye was raised in Youngsville, North Carolina. He is the author of the poetry collections *a little bump in the earth* (Copper Canyon Press, 2024), *Cardinal* (Copper Canyon Press, 2020), and *River Hymns* (American Poetry Review, 2017), winner of the APR/Honickman First Book Prize. A Cave Canem fellow and a Palm Beach Poetry Festival Langston Hughes Fellow, Daye is the recipient of a Whiting Writers Award, a Kate Tufts Award finalist, and a 2021 Paterson Prize finalist. He was the 2019 Diana and Simon Raab Writer-In-Residence at the University of California, Santa Barbara, and received an Amy Clampitt Residency. Daye is an Assistant Professor at the University of North Carolina at Chapel Hill.

Heather Frese's debut novel, *The Baddest Girl on the Planet*, won the Lee Smith Novel Prize. Her second book, *The Saddest Girl on the Beach*, is its companion novel. Her work has been published widely, earning notable mentions in the *Pushcart Prize Anthology* and *Best American Essays*. She received her master's degree from Ohio University and her M.F.A. from West Virginia University. Coastal North Carolina is her longtime love and source of inspiration, her writing deeply influenced by the wild magic and history of the Outer Banks. She currently writes, edits, and teaches in Raleigh, North Carolina.

Julie Funderburk is the author of the poetry collection *The Door That Always Opens* (Louisiana State University Press, 2016) and the chapbook *Thoughts to Fold into Birds* (Unicorn Press, 2014). Her poetry appears in *Blackbird, The Southern Review, Ecotone, SWING,* and *Pleiades.* The recipient of fellowships from the North Carolina Arts Council and the Sewanee Writers' Conference, she teaches at Queens University in Charlotte, North Carolina.

Jeremy B. Jones is the author of the nonfiction book *Cipher: Decoding My Ancestor's Scandalous Secret Diaries* (Blair, 2025) as well as the memoir *Bearwallow: A Personal History of a Mountain Homeland* (Blair, 2014). *Bearwallow* was named the 2014 Appalachian Book of the Year in nonfiction and was awarded gold in the 2015 Independent Publisher Book (IPPY) Awards in memoir. His essays have been published in *Oxford American*, *Garden & Gun*, *The Bitter Southerner*, and *Brevity*, among others. He also writes frequently for *Our State Magazine*. Jeremy earned his MFA from the University of Iowa and is a professor of English Studies at Western Carolina University, in his native North Carolina. He also serves as the series co-editor for In Place: a literary nonfiction book series from WVU Press.

Mark Powell is the author of nine novels, including *Small Treasons*—a SIBA Okra Pick, and a Southern Living Best Book of the Year—and *Lioness*. He has received fellowships from the National Endowment for the Arts, the Breadloaf and Sewanee Writers' Conferences, and twice from the Fulbright Foundation to Slovakia and Romania. In 2009, he received the Chaffin Award for contributions to Appalachian literature. He has written about Southern culture and music for the *Oxford American*, the war in Ukraine for *The Daily Beast*, and his dog for *Garden & Gun*. He holds degrees from the Citadel, the University of South Carolina, and Yale Divinity School, and directs the creative writing program at Appalachian State University.

Amy Rowland is the author of two novels, *The Transcriptionist* (Algonquin, 2014) and *Inside the Wolf* (Algonquin, 2023). Her short fiction is in *The Iowa Review*, *The Southern Review*, *EPOCH*, *New Letters*, and elsewhere. She teaches at UC Berkeley.

Julia Ridley Smith is the author of a short story collection, *Sex Romp Gone Wrong*, and a memoir, *The Sum of Trifles*, about cleaning out her antique-dealer parents' house, grief, and what the objects we live with mean to us. Smith's short stories and essays have appeared in *The Cincinnati Review*, *Ecotone*, *The Missouri Review*, *New England Review*, and *The Southern Review*, among other publications, and her work has been recognized as notable in *Best American Essays*. She teaches creative writing at UNC Chapel Hill. Find her at juliaridleysmith.com.

Zackary Vernon is an associate professor of English at Appalachian State University. His work has appeared in a range of magazines and journals, including *The Bitter Southerner*, *Carolina Quarterly*, and *Southern Cultures*, and he has received both the Alex Albright Creative Nonfiction Prize and the Randall Kenan Prize from the *North Carolina Literary Review*. His debut novel *Our Bodies Electric* was published in 2024.

Ross White is the director of Bull City Press, an independent publisher of poetry, fiction, and nonfiction. He is the author of *Charm Offensive*, winner of the Sexton Prize for Poetry, and three chapbooks: *How We Came Upon the Colony*, *The Polite Society*, and *Valley of Want*. His poems have appeared in *American Poetry Review*, *New England Review*, *POETRY*, *Ploughshares*, *Poetry Daily*, and *The Southern Review*, among others. He teaches creative writing at the University of North Carolina at Chapel Hill and cohosts *The Chapbook*, a podcast devoted to tiny, delightful collections.

www.ingramcontent.com/pod-product-compliance
Lightning Source LLC
Jackson TN
JSHW081721030226
97352JS00001B/1
* 9 7 8 1 9 5 8 8 8 8 6 5 0 *